THE GOBLIN'S BRIDE

A FEUD SO DARK AND LOVELY BOOK ONE

LEIGH KELSEY

LYSANDRA GLASS

www.leighkelsey.co.uk

Want an email when new books release?

Join Lysandra's newsletter

Join Leigh's newsletter for 4 freebies

Or keep up with news on Facebook:

Follow Lysandra on Facebook

Or chat with Leigh in her Facebook group, Leigh Kelsey's Paranormal Den

Cover by https://www.creya-tive.com/

❀ Created with Vellum

BLURB

Marry him. Kiss him. Kill him. But never love him.

The goblin prince killed my sister. For years, I've waited for justice, and I've finally found the perfect opportunity: Kier Kollastus, the prince himself, will agree to peace with his human enemies if a sacrifice is given. A human bride.

With my face veiled and my knives hidden, I offer myself as the prince's sacrifice, wearing a liar's smile as I wait to cut his throat when he sleeps.

But Kier is indestructible except for one night every year. And worse—he's not the barbarian goblins are supposed to be. He's almost ... appealing. If I'm not careful, I'll lose my head.

Or my traitor heart.

The Goblin's Bride is an enemies-to-lovers fantasy romance with a revenge-sworn heroine and a brooding goblin prince. Expect sizzling tension and a dark mystery that lovers of Hades & Persephone and Beauty & The Beast will enjoy.

THE
GOBLIN'S
BRIDE

LEIGH KELSEY
LYSANDRA GLASS

NOTE

Marrying a goblin and plotting a murder is not a recommended replacement for therapy.

*T*he barracks were full of shouting and the delightful scent of a hundred trainees sweating at once. I leaned on the stone balcony overlooking the training yard, the crooked rooftops of Seagrave like dried blood under the baking midday sun. Below, charcoal-black uniforms spread as far as I could see, filling the walled-in acres around the barracks with grunts of exertion and cries of victory.

"I should be down there training with them," I fumed for the ninth time today. Or the nine-hundredth.

"Letta," Adellina hissed, dark eyes widening in her tanned face as she turned to me. "Don't let Celandine hear you say that."

I rolled my eyes, less because her warning was valid than because I was sick to death of Celandrine. I was *special*, one of the lucky ones—the shining bloody stars of the Lucrecian army.

We trained in enclosed indoor chambers with the best tutors the kingdom had to offer in noble arts and courtly battle, kept safely away from the messy sprawl of the training yard. We weren't prepared for battle, but to be propped on a warhorse and paraded among the women and men on the ground—the *real* army—to give them something worth fighting for.

I'd joined the army for revenge, but they'd made me a fucking figurehead.

I didn't want to gallop among the sweaty, blood-stained ranks in clean armour, safely shielded from the gruesome reality of war. I wanted to be in the thick of it, to unleash myself upon every goblin bastard on the other side until I found *him*.

The goblin prince. My sister's murderer.

Then I'd cast off every fencing and politics lesson and reveal the scrappy street rat, thief, and assassin I'd been before Celandrine made me one of her shining soldiers.

I'd given it a lot of thought; what I'd do when I saw the goblin prince. I'd vault off my glorious bloody horse—not *literally* bloody, gods forbid—and land in the muck in front of the goblin bastard. While he was caught off guard, I'd throw my fist into his solar plexus, drive my knee into his dick, and smash his head against my knee for good measure. When he was disoriented, I'd pluck out his eyes and teeth and make a damn necklace of them.

I might have forgotten to mention I was a *tad* unbalanced.

Growing up on the salt-stained, crime infested streets of Seagrave will do that to a girl. You grow up fast, or you don't grow up at all.

"Letta," Adellina said, making me jump when she laid a hand on my shoulder. The blonde figurehead-in-training should have known better than to touch someone as unbalanced as me, but she suited this life in a way I never would. She didn't know the wildness that sank into your bones when you had to fight for scraps of food and a safe place to sleep for the night.

She wasn't like me and Natasya, homeless when our uncle died, penniless at twelve and sixteen. Adellina had grown up in a warm, homely place where she'd never had to feel the awful, weakening gnaw of hunger. I tried not to resent her for it, but it wasn't easy.

"I'm coming," I said absently, but I wasn't really on this balcony looking at the training soldiers.

No, I was on a run-down street at the edge of the city, running so fast I got cuts on my feet through my too-thin shoes, with breath scraping my throat with every gasp I took. Natasya had been gone for five weeks then, fighting the brutal war between humans and the goblin bastards who kept trying to steal our land.

I'd had no proof the rumours were about her, that the whispers of a brutalised, shredded body dumped on the edge of the city was my sister. I couldn't have known, but it didn't stop me running as fast as I could.

The sight of her body when I'd found her, surrounded by gossip-hounds and onlookers... There was no erasing that sort of image.

As gruesome as her body was, she could have been anyone. But the blood-covered necklace around her shredded throat was unmistakable: a simple chain with five teardrops in hammered gold. It was mum's, the only thing Uncle Tavish let us keep when he inherited us along with her belongings. Dick.

I might not have known who'd killed Natasya if I hadn't heard the gossiping woman beside me ramble to her friend about how she'd seen him stalk up to the city and dump the body on the border. Tall and horrific with ice-blue muscle, he had long black hair and teeth like a thousand needles.

Everyone knew Kier Kollastus, one of three Goblin Princes. Every human knew to run the other way when they saw him.

I touched the necklace hanging around my throat, tracing the shape of the teardrops.

"I'll make him pay, Natasya," I whispered, barely loud enough for the wind to hear.

I had nothing left, the only family I loved gone, and no one close enough to consider a friend. But I had revenge, and it burned hot enough to keep me warm on freezing nights.

I might not have been down on the training grounds, but I'd find a way onto the battlefield, and I'd shred that bastard goblin like he'd shredded my sister.

"Whatever it takes," I promised, "the Goblin Prince is dead."

"*O*ne more comment, and I'm going to shove this pretty sword through her throat," I hissed, my teeth bared as Celandrine barked corrections and insults from her perch at the far end of the room.

The sword was a joke, barely more than a flimsy metal ribbon, with a mess of swirling strands around the handle to protect my hand. In a real fight, it would snap in a heartbeat, and I'd have to rely on the daggers and throwing stars hidden in my navy blue dress.

Not that Celandrine knew they were there.

I swung my flimsy sword hard enough that it nearly embedded in the dummy I was training with.

"Not so rough, Zabaletta," she called from the throne-like chair she sat on, elevated so she could watch her twelve acolytes practise pretty war. We didn't need to *really* fight, only to look like we could so we'd inspire the mud-splattered, wound-burdened masses.

Her last crop of figureheads had gone out to the field last week, decked out in expensive clothes and freshly hammered armour, shining like fire under the watery

Seagrave sun. I could almost forget they were riding through foul-smelling streets, the pompous, benevolent looks on their faces akin to a royal's composure. They didn't seem to care that the people reaching out to touch their horses were stained with grime and salt and a hard day's work.

That was my future; smiling like a brain dead moron, parading riches and gold and useless bloody swords past the people of Seagrave.

If Celandrine hadn't promised me revenge for joining her pathetic little band, I'd have been watching the parade with a sneer on my face. There was plenty of work in Seagrave if you were willing to play by darker rules; anyone could make a living as a thief, fence, assassin, mercenary, or pirate.

I should have been out there, back in my old life, but I clung to Celandrine's promise. She was one of four generals in Seagrave, and one of eleven in the kingdom of Lucre. If anyone could get me to Kier Kollastus, it was her.

I jammed the razor end of my sword through the dummy, stuffing and feathers exploding out the other end. Teeth gritted with satisfaction, I imagined it was my first move against the goblin prince who'd slaughtered my sister.

I wrenched it out to take another stab, but I hissed when Celandrine shouted, "Zabaletta, take a break."

I spun, blood roaring in my ears, but I knew by the narrow-eyed warning on her perfect onyx face that it wasn't a suggestion.

My heart thumped as loud as the sea, but I sketched a sardonic bow and ignored the looks burning my shoulders as I aimed for the door. Sometimes I *hated* this place with its elegance and gilt-edges on every damn thing. Why did a chamber pot need gilt edges for fuck's sake? Everything reminded me of how different things were now than before, when Natasya had been alive.

In my clearer moments, I knew I was taking my grief out on Celandrine and the other figureheads. I knew they didn't exactly deserve it, since every single person here had a story like mine—one to make our soldiers furious, to remind them why they should fight. *Everyone* had a slaughtered sister, or a tortured father, or a mother brutalised in ways so horrific words weren't yet invented. But I couldn't rein in my anger.

My footsteps slapped the marble under me with punishing blows, my blood still pounding too fast, too loud. It was so loud that I couldn't hear myself think. It blotted out the conversations of people I passed—Celandrine's younger acolytes, the staff who kept the barracks running, and the real soldiers who lived in the lower floors. But my steps stumbled when a loud trumpet call cut through even my pounding blood.

I froze, all the motion in the corridor halting around me. I locked eyes with a black-clad soldier carrying a bundle of arrows and quivers downstairs, a moment of shared panic. Those calls only rang across Seagrave for two reasons: to announce a storm, or to warn of goblins.

I wanted a chance to kill the goblin prince, but I hadn't expected it so soon.

Still, beggars couldn't be choosers.

My blood pumped for an altogether different reason as I spun on my heel and raced for the balcony doors, my skirts rustling around me like churning satin waves. More people streamed out of the doors along the corridor, Adellina sending me a frantic look as she joined my side, her face exceptionally pale.

"What's happening?" she asked, as if I could possibly know.

"I guess we'll find out," I replied grimly, casting a sideways glance at Celandrine as she emerged from the room in a swirl of ivory skirts and pearls, her expression taut with a fierce readiness I hadn't expected to see on her cherubic face.

Maybe I'd been underestimating my tutor a smidge.

A voice rang across the dark red roofs of Seagrave before we even reached the balcony, but amplified as the speaker was by magic—stolen magic—*goblin* magic—there was no mistaking the announcement.

A ceasefire is imminent. Our goblin enemies will retreat into their country in exchange for a human bride for their oldest prince. Volunteers should present themselves at the Merikand tower.

Silence rang as the voice faded, cut only by the trumpet call signifying the end of the message.

Goosebumps covered my arms, not entirely because of the chill sea wind coming through the balcony doors.

"A human bride," Adellina echoed, wrapping her arms around herself with a shudder. "No one in their right mind would marry a goblin."

"Let alone a *prince* of the monsters," another of Celandrine's trainees added in disgust.

Merikand echoed between my ears. The name translated to *land of slaughter.* It was a fitting place for me to murder my sworn enemy.

"Yes," Celandrine agreed in a tight voice, her dark eyes burning through my skull. "No one in their right mind would."

Good thing I'd lost my sanity long ago. I couldn't keep the little smirk off my face as I reformed and reshaped my plan, my heart beating faster and a dangerous thrill in my belly.

I didn't know how I would get to the Merikand outpost, but that didn't matter. I had a goblin to wed and a husband to kill.

"Why are you smiling?" Adellina asked in alarm.

I patted my almost-friend's arm as I turned, avoiding Celandrine's knowing stare. "No reason, Adellina. No reason at all."

3

"What a joke," I laughed under my breath, easily sneaking out of the barracks and disappearing into the shadow-wrapped streets of Seagrave. The security was pitiful, all their attention on stopping people creeping *in* instead of breaking *out*.

It wasn't like I was a prisoner anyway; Celandrine was happy for us to go shopping at the market or to visit family, but sneaking out to marry a goblin prince? Something told me my permission form would get a giant red cross through it.

I kept my steps light and soundless as I followed the high brick wall around the barracks, the salt-laced air tasting different than it had earlier. It was good to be back in my black leathers, the weight of my familiar weapons a comfort at my hips, thigh, and inside the sleeves of my ribbed jacket. I couldn't turn up at the Merikand outpost looking like an assassin, but I'd make the most of it while I could.

Part of me wanted to drop by my old attic in Marc the Scythe's building and scare the shit out of whatever little tyrant had my room now. Whatever scrappy, grief-filled kid he was training up now.

Anyone else might have resented what the Scythe had made me into, but without his tutorage, without him giving me training to focus on, I don't know what I'd have done after I lost Natasya. And not the soft, gentile training Celandrine inflicted on me; *real* training, with blood, sweat, and dirty tactics.

I scaled a familiar pipe around the back of an inn owned by two dealers in the Scythe's network, silent feet carrying me across the roof.

"Oh, I missed you," I whispered to my rubber slippers. My feet constantly ached from being jammed into heels, but there was nothing quite like the sensation of roof tiles beneath my feet, the unerring grip of the rubber as I leapt from the inn to a gold merchant's shop to a slaughterhouse.

The wind whistled past my ears, sharp air filling my lungs, and I swore my blood sang. I was alive again after so long shoved into a stifling role.

I wasn't sweet and pristine and shining, a glowing symbol of valour. I was rough and violent and not very nice, and it felt damn good to be reminded of that.

Maybe, if the goblins hadn't agreed to a ceasefire in exchange for a bride, I would have stayed with Celandrine and become a true figurehead. Maybe I'd have ridden out in battle after battle, primped and gleaming, a ribbon streaming from my helmet, until I finally found the goblin who slaughtered my sister.

Marrying him was far sweeter.

My heart thumped with eagerness as I leapt across a wider distance, the fraught moment between falling and catching myself on the eaves of the bakery making blood pound in my ears. It was an addictive feeling, the rush, the uncertainty—the fall.

The edge of the city grew nearer, the hollow thumps of boat hulls knocking together fading as I jumped across rooftops, my heart beating fast and sure.

I let myself picture the moment when I would kill the prince. We'd already be married at that point; maybe he'd fall asleep in the carriage spiriting us across the border into goblin lands and I'd drag my dagger across his throat, nice and slow.

In my fantasy, blood spilled over his vile blue throat, as violently red as any human's blood. I shuddered hard enough that I nearly missed my next catch. I swore sharply at myself, dragging myself onto the roof of a crooked terrace house with gloved, shaky hands.

I panted there, the wind tugging red hair from my pony-tail, and I didn't know if I was shaky because of the near-fall or because of the fantasy.

"Maybe I'll have to go along with the marriage until we're back at his home," I whispered, staring across the last few rows of houses to the border where Natasya's gruesome body had been dumped.

"Maybe I'll wait until he's sleeping," I went on, breathing faster, my heart churning with hatred. "He'll never know I'm there to kill him until it's too late."

With that thought ringing through the night, I jumped across the last few houses and landed nimbly on the stretch of empty land at the border. I checked all my knives were in place, tightened my ponytail, and pulled my black scarf over my mouth as I set off across the vast lands.

There were endless miles and six cities between Seagrave on the ocean and Merikand on the edge of the goblin lands. At least four days' walk, even at a revenge-fuelled pace.

Four days, and then I'd avenge Natasya. Four days and the goblin prince would be dead.

"I'm almost there, Natasya," I breathed, crunching grass under my rubber shoes. "Almost there."

4

"*L*ook, sweetheart," I sighed, gesturing with my scratched, well-loved dagger, "I don't *want* to stab you. You've clearly gone to a lot of effort to beautify yourself, and you look lovely. That hair? I'm in awe. And I have serious make-up envy. But I need the dress, okay?"

The beautiful, bronze-skinned woman shook, her hands raised in a plea I couldn't answer, no matter how pretty she was. "Don't hurt me."

"Then get stripping, honey," I replied, trying to be soft. It didn't come naturally, but I needed to practise if I was going to convince whoever stood between me and marrying Kier Kollastus.

Would there be an interview process? An audition? I didn't know, but I'd make damn sure I was the only viable option.

I leaned against a glossy wooden counter in the dressmaker's shop I'd commandeered, and gave the fearful woman a hurry up gesture.

We were alone, courtesy of the rag soaked in sleeproot I'd pressed to the shop owner's mouth. She was laid on the ground behind the counter having a nice nap. I did feel a *little* bad about that, but she'd be fine. And I'd have a dress to wear to my wedding.

The shaky woman—something flowy and feminine like Laurel or Willow—inhaled a wobbly breath and pulled her long, seafoam-green dress over her head. It was completely sheer, with flowers trapped between layers of tulle, and a plain shift underneath it protected her modesty. It was also the only dress suitable for a wedding that didn't require help to fasten the masochistic arrangement of stays and corseting beautiful women tended to wear. Pity that someone else had already been wearing it when I got here.

Corseting was another thing I'd have to get used to to keep up this ruse. Ugh. How long would I have to play at being the sweet, sacrificial bride? How long until the goblin prince's blood dirtied my knife?

"Thanks *so* much," I said as the woman dropped the gauzy fabric to the floor and stepped out of it. "And the shift," I added.

She squeaked, her dark eyes wide with horror.

I sighed, and proved how decent a human being I was by grabbing a pastel dress from a nearby rail and throwing it to Laurel. Clover. Flora. Something like that.

"I won't peek at your exciting bits, don't worry," I assured her. "My eyes will stay firmly neck-up."

I flashed her a smile I meant to be reassuring, but judging by the way her throat bobbed, it may have been more wolfish than planned.

She shimmied out of the white shift in record time, shakily pulling up the floral dress I'd stolen from the rack.

"Much obliged," I purred, and stripped off my black leather, ignoring her squeak of surprise at my nudity.

I pulled on the shift and then the gauzy, floral garment,

trying not to wince when I shoved my feet into the toe-pinching silk shoes I'd pilfered from the back of the shop. A size too small, but they'd do.

"How do I look?" I asked the terrified woman, giving her a twirl. "Do I look bride-ish?"

"I-I think so," she whispered, her hands shaking as she twisted them in front of her, taking a hesitant step back.

"Not the most glowing compliment," I remarked, "but I'll take it. Oh, Willow?"

"Orchid," she corrected breathlessly, freezing as my attention settled fully on her.

"Orchid," I amended with a smile, grabbing the rag from where I'd left it on the counter.

I rushed across the distance between me and the beautiful woman before she could flee.

"I *need* to marry that prince, so I can't let you present yourself at the tower. Sorry, Orchid," I added genuinely as she slumped with a soft cry.

I caught her as she fell, lowering her gently to the ground. She'd be unconscious for a day or two, but with no lasting effects.

"You're better off without a goblin for a husband," I assured her, patting her shoulder. "He doesn't deserve you."

But me? I was *exactly* what Kier Kollastus deserved.

With a last look at the unconscious would-be bride and the dressmaker, I made sure my wedding dress covered my weapons, and headed out the door.

The sun was just starting to set over the town, staining the high street orange and red. Merikand had been prosperous and elegant once, but the war had made it a dust-covered shell of its former glory. Maybe when I killed the prince, the goblins' army would fall apart, and Merikand could be rebuilt.

That'd be a lovely little bonus to jamming my knife in his throat.

The wedding was scheduled for dawn. No matter what I had to do in the dark hours of the night to ensure it, I would be the one standing at the altar across from my sister's killer.

"Good luck," a round-faced woman called when she spotted me leaving the dressmaker's shop, thinking me as guileless and sacrificing as Orchid.

"Thanks," I replied with a grin, throwing my shoulders back and crossing the cracked road.

Time to find the next bride and give them a taste of sleeproot.

5

"Well isn't *this* pretty?" I remarked, about to lean against the side of the tower of Merikand before I remembered the pale green dress I wore. I wouldn't look very bridal with a dirty big smear down my backside.

"*So* kind of you to string such lovely lights in the trees for me," I said under my breath, surveying the wedding site.

There were only twelve chairs on either side of the petal-strewn aisle, wrapped in white cloth and tied with gauzy bows, but there'd already been hundreds of spectators pressed against the fence around the tower when I arrived at the gates.

The guards had been stunned; with dawn approaching and no bride presented at the gates, they'd been more than relieved to see me. Of course, they didn't know I was the reason everyone else had come down with a sudden case of unconsciousness or sickness, or misplaced their dresses, or found themselves locked in a room with no way out.

I'd had a busy night, and I was exhausted, but the thought of revenge made me buzz with energy.

I lifted my gaze from the frothy white chairs when footsteps scraped the dirt near the tower. They were idiots to leave me unattended in such an important military outpost, but I didn't look like an assassin or thief right now. I didn't even look like one of Celandrine's shining, armour-plated figureheads.

"Nikoli," I said with a cheery smile, greeting the young guard. He was greener than a field of goblin's bane, with a teenager's face despite his shaved head and a passing attempt at a mean scowl.

"The paperwork's ready," he said, clearing his throat when his voice came out gruff and thick. I got the impression I unsettled him; probably because I kept smiling like a fox with a mouse when I should have been wringing my hands and fretting about marrying our enemy.

Note to self: pretend to be afraid as well as sweet and guileless.

"So it's time?" I asked, lowering my voice to a thready whisper.

His baby face softened, sympathy entering dark brown eyes, and I mentally patted myself on the back for the performance. I wanted a shiny brass award for this role.

I made a show of raising myself to my full height and nodding at Nikoli, while inside I was doing cartwheels. My stomach twisted and fluttered as Nikoli held out his hand, gesturing for me to follow him out of the shadow of the tower and through a nondescript door.

Soon, I would say my vows and look my sister's killer in the eye. But now, I had a banal document to sign.

Nikoli watched me as he led me down a curving hallway that smelled of blood and metal, and into a room that contained two people—a general in her prime and an ageing archivist who would witness my signature.

I surveyed the room as subtly as possible. It was bare except for a couple bookcases and a heavy oak desk with a green lamp. An attempt at décor had been made with a single tulip in a vase on the windowsill behind the desk, but it did little to make the bland room homely.

Should I have been excited? Because every step I took across the polished floorboards to the pen that waited for me, to the people who watched me with sad, mournful expressions, made me giddy.

"We thank you for your service," the general said, bowing her dark head to me, her sharp bob of hair swinging around her chin. "What's your name?"

I could have lied. Probably should have. But I wanted them to know exactly who'd killed the goblin bastard, so I replied, "Zabaletta Stellara."

"I'm General Ovinia. This is Andros Huda—he'll oversee your signature and make sure the documents are properly filed."

She paused, something heavy in the breath she took. I wanted to tell her it was no big deal, I was fine. But I couldn't risk them finding out why I was really here and sabotaging my big day.

"There's no preparing you for marriage to a goblin," she said gravely, crossing her arms over her black-fatigue-clad chest. Gods, the woman was covered in muscle; her arms bulged distractingly and I had to tear my eyes away. "There's been no record of it in the human lands, and any who've gone to their country to marry haven't returned to tell the tales."

Ooh, I'd be the first to come back with a grizzly marriage story? Maybe I'd write a book; I bet publishers would clamour to print it. I could be rich.

I caught my grin just before it formed and stamped it out, nodding solemnly at General Ovinia.

"Be careful," she added, still watching me like a crab she was about to throw into a boiling pot of water. She thought my fate was to become soup—and I'd make one hell of a delicious soup—but if I *was* a crab, I'd be clamping my pincers on someone's face and ripping their nose off.

"I will," I lied, with all the severity of a promise. "I know what I'm getting myself into, General. But it's for the good of Lucre." Weaving a bit of truth to legitimise myself, I added, "My sister died for this war. It needs to end."

"It *does*," the archivist agreed fiercely. Andros Huda. I'd heard of him, but never thought I'd meet the guy. He once wrote a scathing piece about Celandrine and pissed her all the way off. I lowkey wanted to shake his hand, but I had to stay in character.

"If you're ready," the general said with a smile softening the brutal edges of her face, "you can sign the marriage contract."

And end it at the earliest possible chance by taking advantage of that cute little clause; 'til death do us part.

Death would do us part alright. When I'd finished with Kier Kollastus, there wouldn't be enough left of him to send to whatever afterlife the goblins believed in.

Adrenaline made me tremble as I picked up the heavy pen and scrawled my name in the empty spot. His was already dry on the paper, taunting me with the elegance of his handwriting. I dug a little too hard into the paper, and lifted the pen quickly with a wince. It hadn't ripped, thank fuck.

"So it's done," Andros said grimly when I stepped back.

Would it be rude to keep the pen as a souvenir? I subtly slid it toward my sleeve, but Andros absently took it from my hand and checked the ink was dry before rolling up the contract. I tried not to pout at him stealing my pen.

"Right then," General Ovinia said, clasping my shoulder and making me jump. It was an effort not to stab her, or at least punch her in the kidney.

Not too rough, Celandrine would have chided me back at the barracks. It was fucking typical that I'd left that life behind and her criticisms were haunting me.

"All that's left to do is exchange your vows."

General Ovinia squeezed my shoulder, a comforting touch that reminded me of Natasya. Inconvenient. I shut off the emotions as much as I could, reminding myself of the weapons hidden under my dress and the goblin who would be dead by midnight.

"I'm ready," I replied, after discarding a half dozen replies. *Bring it on* didn't have the right ring to it. *Lead me to my victim* definitely wasn't right.

Butterflies of nerves and excitement took flight in my belly as they handed me a veil and led me out the door with a murmur that this would be a quick ceremony, nothing to be afraid of. I noticed no one suggested the marriage itself was nothing to be afraid of.

I imagined Orchid, harmless and anxious, walking down this long corridor towards her goblin groom. She'd have been trembling, struggling to master her breathing. I was doing everyone a favour by making sure I was the bride. At least none of the other women would be pressed into a love-less, terror-ruled marriage.

Why had Orchid wanted to marry Kier Kollastus anyway? Because she'd been told to by her family? Greed could do cruel things to people, even to parents. A goblin prince was still a prince, and came with all the money and power of a human royal. Or had Orchid come here out of the goodness of her heart?

That's how I'd write this long walk down the tower aisle when I penned my memoir; I'd write myself as a gallant saviour, sparing the other women from a cruel goblin. At least none of them would be shredded to ribbons and dumped on the edge of their city. I was here for selfish reasons, but at least that was some good to come out of it.

Well, that and Kier's heart being carved out of his body. My murder fantasies were growing more elaborate with every step I took.

I kept my gaze forward as General Ovinia gave me a last squeeze and fell back, Andros alongside her. The air smelled exactly how I'd expected a border town to: of gunpowder and metal and blood, with an underlying scent of burning meat. It fit the theme of my wedding perfectly, not that anyone else knew it would end in death.

Natasya had been out here, fighting in the miles ahead of the tower—that wasteland between human and goblin lands. It hadn't always been a wasteland; it had been a trading metropolis two hundred years ago, where both species coexisted peacefully. It was impossible to imagine that now.

Maybe in the afterworld, this spit of land was still full of traders and markets full of rich spices, luxurious fabrics, and jewellery so gold it looked like the craftsmen had melted the sun. Maybe Natasya was there, happy and at peace.

Or maybe she was suffering in an endless world of torture and shredded flesh, living her death over and over. For that, I'd make today count.

6

I dragged a slow breath through my nostrils as I took measured steps down the petal-strewn aisle. I couldn't even smell the sweetness of the flowers over the stink of the battlefield mere miles ahead. It was a reminder of why this wedding was happening, why we were really here. Not for a love match, or a happy occasion. For war.

I didn't think a human bride would end the war, and I certainly didn't think peace would last when I killed Kier, but if anyone thought a wedding would fix a two centuries old feud, they were delusional.

Why a bride? Why was *that* the goblins' price for stopping the war? I should have asked the general when I'd had the chance, instead of getting caught up in my gore-strewn fantasies.

Voices rose and hummed around me the closer I got to the seats at the end of the aisle. The closer I got to the gold-robed holy woman and my heinous future husband.

I tried not to look at him. No matter my plan, no matter how many years I'd dreamed and planned the moment of his death, if I looked at him, I'd lose it. He'd shredded my sister's body like she was fucking *mincemeat*, and my rage was a living thing inside me, a burning sun just behind my ribcage.

Sweat trickled down the groove of my spine as I walked, clouds drifting aside to let the sun roast me inside my tulle and lace. Gods, please don't let there be sweat stains. I could handle a lot of things, but after the trouble I'd gone through to steal this dress, the last thing I wanted was the humiliation of yellow patches under my arms.

Blood stains? Sign me the fuck up. But anything even *remotely* yellow? Gods, no.

"Poor thing," someone murmured to the witness sitting beside them, all of them likely higher-ups—commanders, politicians, governors, and ladies.

"How long do you suppose she'll last?" someone else asked.

I couldn't resist flashing them a fierce, teeth-baring smile. "Longer than you would, I'd wager," I replied, shocking the red-faced man into shamed silence. Good. I was a worldly assassin with life skills and street smarts; I didn't give a shit what they said about me. But they'd have said the same thing about poor Orchid, and that rankled.

If I really *had* been offered as a sacrifice to a violent husband who could easily kill me, they'd have gossiped the exact same things. And that pissed me the hell off.

Sharp motion drew my eye exactly where I'd sworn not to look: at the goblin prince. He'd turned at my voice, an expression of surprise on his rugged face—a matching one to my own, I guessed, as I registered the deeply tanned skin, *not* icy blue. His eyes were so sapphire they were almost black, there was scruffy facial hair on his jaw, and long black hair hung down his back.

He didn't look like a goblin. It wouldn't stop me killing

him, but it was a swift reminder of that more deadly weapon goblins possessed: shape-changing. Like this, he could blend in with humans. No sharply pointed ears, no razor claws or needle-like teeth.

Bastard.

Now I shook, tulle rustling around my body as I wrenched my stare back to the aisle and took my next steps. I heard people note the way I trembled and my rapid breathing. I tried to wipe the rage from my expression, but I couldn't quite manage it. Fury bubbled inside me like poison, and I was glad for the veil blurring my features.

I focused on the added weight at my hip, thigh, hidden down my spine, and up my sleeve—my knives.

Three more steps, and I stood beside him, my future husband.

My skin crawled. My hands itched to draw a knife.

I couldn't stop seeing Natasya, slit open in so many places she was unrecognisable—but not by a knife or sword. By *claws*. The claws this bastard hid behind the harmless, handsome guise of a human. As if he'd *ever* be one of us.

Goblins hated humans, wanted to wipe us off the face of the world. The only reason he wasn't monstrous and blue right now was he wanted us to underestimate him.

I refused.

The rough voice of the holy woman made me jump as she lifted her hands to quiet the crowd, her golden robes swaying around her. She looked like every other Lucrecian priest I'd seen: silver-haired, grave-faced, and dull. I'd heard stories of churches in neighbouring countries where they sang their prayers, where worship wasn't droning and full of warnings, omens, and rules. There were no stories about worship in the goblin lands. For all I knew, they worshipped death and held weekly slaughter parties.

"Distinguished guests," the holy woman called. "Bear witness to the momentous marriage of Zabaletta Stellara and Kier Ulysses Kollastus, peace-bringers of our two peoples."

My mouth twitched at the edge, and I hoped the veil blurred my smirk of satisfaction. They'd said my name first. It was petty, listing his name after mine when tradition always placed a groom's name before the bride's, but I got a kick out of it. Besides, why shouldn't I be up front and centre? I was the one sacrificing my life in a show of selflessness and downright saintly patriotism.

Judging by the rustle of silk and leather as my groom shifted his weight, he hadn't missed the slight. And he was pissed by it. Good.

My heart thundered, full of hate. I stayed firm this time, and didn't look at my hateful husband-to-be. This close, I could snap and kill him. Not so smart to commit murder in front of the great powers of Lucre. There'd be no memoirs, no riches, and certainly no future after the murder if I was witnessed.

It'd be fun to see everyone's reaction, though. I imagined their horrified shouts as the fair, harmless bride murdered her groom before vows could be exchanged; the visual kept me sane throughout the holy woman's introduction.

Her words rang through my ears though. Peace-bringers of our two peoples. If these guys thought the peace granted by this marriage would last, they were crazy. I was doing them a favour by taking out their prince. And if I wasn't, I honestly didn't give a shit. He'd slaughtered my sister first; I was just returning the favour by stabbing him.

Or carving out his heart.

Or hacking off his head.

I was keeping my options open.

"Zabaletta," the holy woman said, making me jump. My veiled face prickled with awareness of the prince looking at me, his eyes like knife wounds down my cheek. "Do you dedicate your love and your life to this man?"

I dedicated both to murdering him. That counted, right?

I dragged in a sharp breath and said, "I do."

Pride simmered in the holy woman's eyes, and I pursed my lips. Was she proud of me for whoring myself to a goblin for peace, or proud of herself for her role in the wedding? No doubt her name would be splashed all over the papers tomorrow. Hell, she could probably get her own book deal. Marriage of Monsters: A Priest's Tale. People would buy it.

"Kier," the woman said, turning to him with a more guarded expression. He stiffened, nodding at her. I refused to look at him the way he'd stared at me while I vowed my dedication. "Do you dedicate your love and your life to this woman?"

"I do."

I blinked, tilting my head at the thunderous anger in his voice. Oh, he wasn't happy about this. Then why show up and give his vow? Curiosity made my mind race. There was no way he could know I'd be his bride, so he couldn't have been angry at marrying the sister of one of his victims.

Panic made me jumpy, but I dismissed all my fears. He had no idea what I planned; he could have ended up marrying any of the brides I'd knocked out overnight. He was angry about the wedding itself.

"Zabaletta," the holy woman said to me, her hands still lifted, golden robes fluttering in the foul-smelling wind. "Will you, to the best of your ability, care for this man through light and dark, sickness and health, fortune and mischance?"

Not in a million fucking years.

"I will," I agreed, sweat rolling down my spine. I was glad for the wind, though; it dispelled some of the baking heat until I could breathe clearer. Almost, almost done, and then we'd be alone. And my knife would be in his throat.

But everyone would know it was me.

Fuck.

My plans started to unravel. I had to be clever about it. Go home with him, play along for a day or so—and then make it seem like someone else had murdered him.

"Until death do you part?" the woman asked, the final binding vow.

"Until death do us part," I vowed, swallowing.

Could they hear it in my voice—how hungry I was for his death? How eagerly I anticipated it?

"Kier," the priest said, turning to my hateful groom and repeating the same vow. She didn't give me any strange looks, so I hoped my eagerness had gone unnoticed.

"I will."

His rough voice made my body tense all over, my hands twitching at my sides. Hopefully people would think nerves made me restless, and not pure, unbridled hatred.

One more vow, five tiny words, and it was sealed. My heart thumped harder, and I kept my gaze resolutely forward. Natasya's blood-stained body flashed in my mind, and I held onto the image. I could do this. I almost had. Five years of waiting, training, enduring, plotting, and I was almost there.

"Until death do us part," the goblin prince vowed in a voice seething with rage and resentment.

I inhaled a shuddery breath, the air shifting around us. It was done. We'd said our vows, sworn our love and dedication—ha!—and all that was left was for the holy woman to pronounce us—

A sudden explosion knocked me off my feet, and I went crashing to the petal-strewn dirt.

7

*M*y hand was pressed to my knife in an instant, only tulle and lace between my fingers and a weapon. But in the chaos, my wide-eyed stare landed on Kier Kollastus, more monstrous in his human form than with icy blue skin, and I remembered my goal here. My role.

I flexed my fingers and let go, a shudder of dark premonition skirting down my spine.

"Get them!" General Ovinia's voice boomed further up the aisle, harsh with authority. "I want them in a tower vault within the damn minute!"

My heart raced as I stared at the plume of dust and fire raining down around us. Someone had blown up ... what? The tower still stood, and we weren't close enough to the shops and houses of the village for the explosion to hit any of those buildings. So what was the point?

"A protest," Kier's unwelcome voice sounded close by. "From either your species or mine. A lot of people opposed this marriage. Vocally."

I swallowed, my whole body shaking. He was talking to me. This *vile creature* had the *nerve*—shit, my veil had knocked from my face when I hit the ground. He could see everything playing across my face, every flash of rage and disgust, every clench of my jaw as I ground my teeth.

Think—*think!*

I dragged in a shaky breath, tasting gunpowder and explosives.

"We don't deserve this," I rasped. He didn't have to know the rough quality of my voice came from forcing myself to talk to my sister's murderer. Let him think it was fear.

Kier's next breath was a laugh. He didn't bother responding.

"Announce the marriage," Andros Huda boomed at the holy woman crouched on the ground across from us with her arms around her head. The archivist hurried towards us, his head low and his expression blazing with anger.

Another explosion rocked the ground, and I flinched, ducking closer to the dirt on instinct. But the tower didn't collapse, and there was nothing out here near the killing field but grass and dust and dirt. If they were trying to destroy anything, it was *us*—me and my bastard husband.

Sharp, jarring pops of gunfire cut the heavy, muffled quiet and I hissed through my teeth. All I had was steel on me; no guns of my own to defend myself. They were a messy, complicated business I'd never bothered to learn when I could as easily kill someone with a dagger as I could with powder and iron balls.

I was used to hearing shots in Seagrave—where there were gangs and criminals, there were guns—but explosions? Another one erupted, and I couldn't hold back a flinch. The sound crawled inside my skin and made me shake, on edge.

The priest dragged in a shaky breath and yelled out, "I pronounce you married, until your souls turn to dust."

"Good," Andros sighed, sounding relieved. I wondered who he'd lost to the war; for him to have such a big stake in my marriage, it had to be someone pretty important to him.

"So it's done," Kier muttered, sounding about as blissfully happy to be married as I was.

Fear not, I wanted to tell him, *soon you'll be free of your vows.*

I let my fingers glance over the knife at my thigh for reassurance, a trickle of air reaching my lungs until gunshots sounded louder—closer.

I needed to get out of here. If this was Seagrave, I'd be up on the rooftops and clambering across the city to safety, but out here with only the tower as a shield?

I'd known the wedding wouldn't bring eternal peace, but I'd expected it to last longer than two fucking seconds. At least it left the way open for Kier's murder. And butterflies churned in my stomach when I realised I could blame these protesters for his death.

Things were shaping up nicely. But I had to get out of this place first.

"We can't stay here," I hissed to Andros, belatedly remembering my role. The bride I was pretending to be would be terrified and cowed. And the annoying thing was I *was* afraid—I was just used to being scared, and I knew being angry could crush the fear. Luckily, I had an endless supply of anger I could call on.

I pushed off the ground, petals crushed into my palms, and I scanned the dust clouds around us for figures. The obvious plan was to hide in the tower, but it was only a matter of time before the protesters targeted it with their explosives.

I jumped when sky blue light burst from Kier's direction, and I narrowed my eyes in suspicion as he pressed on a cobalt jewel pinned to the lapel of his black suit. Black, not white, I realised. Not even an elegant cream or a daring salmon pink. No, black—black of the void, of hell's darkest pit. Was it an intentional smear on the wedding? A display of how reluctant he was to be my groom?

Well tough shit, now we were married. There was no escaping except by death.

I'd married my sister's killer.

Even though it had been the plan since the moment I heard the announcement, I couldn't help the twist of sickness in my belly. I was married to him—bound by law.

There was no escaping for me, either.

"Xiona," Kier growled at the glowing gem on his collar. "Get me the hell out of here before the rebels blow me up."

I jumped at the sly female voice that rang from the gem, tinny and distant. "And what about your blushing bride?"

"Her, too," Kier ground out.

I bristled, my nostrils flaring, instinctively pushing back against the idea of this monster taking me anywhere.

You're his wife, I reminded myself, which didn't calm the flow of rage making my vision as crimson as blood.

You have to go with him to kill him later, I pointed out, and nodded at my own point. I was right.

I took a rough breath until my shoulders loosened, until my rage thinned—and flinched at another explosion, close enough that my ears rang.

A firm hand coiled around my wrist and tugged me to my feet. I stumbled, finding my balance with difficulty as the gauze-wrapped seats blurred past, the witnesses of my wedding hiding behind them, as if the thin wood would be much protection. It took me far too long to realise the fingers gripping my wrist belonged to Kier Kollastus, and I hissed a warning as he dragged me up the aisle and away from the tower.

I wrenched on his grip, trembling hard at the proximity, at his skin on my skin. I couldn't do this—pretend to be okay with the wedding, pretend I was a normal bride, pretend I didn't want his body as cold as night and six feet under the earth.

"My friends are bringing a carriage," he threw over his shoulder, refusing to let go as he marched me around the back of the tower and away from the sharp pops of gunfire. "They'll get us out of here."

His friends. So I'd be outnumbered. Surrounded by goblins. And trapped in a carriage.

My heart beat faster, the urge to run making my skin stretch tight over my bones. I pulled on the prince's grip again, but he refused to relinquish my wrist.

I couldn't decide what was worse; staying here in the midst of explosions or being locked in a carriage with my husband and his no doubt equally murderous friends.

"Here," Kier rumbled, giving me a yank when a glossy, lacquered black carriage hurtled around the side of the tower, some insignia I didn't recognise on the doors. "Get in. You'll be safe."

I laughed, couldn't hope to contain the burst of bitter sound.

Kier didn't even blink at the laugh. The carriage door slammed open before the wheels had even stopped spinning, and he shoved me up and inside it before I could blink.

In a matter of seconds, I was thrust into a tight space with my sister's killer, and my head spun too fast for me to process the moment, to take advantage of it and end his vile life.

My ears were still ringing from the explosions when he slammed the door shut and the carriage lurched into a sprint, carrying me from the tower, from Merikand, and from the human lands.

a low whistle made me jump, and I wrenched my panicked stare from the wasteland racing past the carriage to the predators who sat inside it with me.

Kier sat as far as possible from me on the same padded bench seat, his face set in a terrifying expression and his tanned hands clenched into fists in his lap. His expensive black suit was streaked with dirt and dust, a smear of it on his jaw. He certainly looked capable of the gruesome murder he'd inflicted on my sister.

I dragged air into my lungs, dropping my gaze before he could glimpse my hate.

"You've done well, Kier," a woman laughed—the same sly voice I'd heard through the gem on his collar. I didn't know what kind of goblin magic powered it, and I didn't want to know. I was already at enough of a disadvantage.

I carefully eyed the two goblins across from me, using every bit of control I had to keep my expression shell-shocked. I couldn't appear sweet and happily married even if I wanted to; stunned was the best I could do.

The woman who'd spoken was striking and beautiful,

with exceptionally long honey-blond hair, golden cheek-bones sharper than my knives, amber eyes winged with dark kohl, and a wicked smirk. She looked like someone I could get along with, if she hadn't been a goblin and friends with Natasya's killer.

"She's hot," she stage-whispered to the goblin prince. He grunted a noncommittal reply.

My attention slid to the other person in the carriage, lounging in the corner with his foot balanced on his opposite knee, casual and languid. Brown-skinned and beautiful, he was as different in appearance to Kier as possible. Black locs were pulled into a messy knot, gold glinted at a piercing in his nose, and his eyes were sultry and warm as they gave me a similar perusal.

"Hello, brideling," he purred, low enough to make my heart skip. Carnal suggestion and deadly power seeped from his voice, and I sat up straighter, painfully aware of how in danger I was right now.

"Really, Rook?" Kier growled, slumping into the corner of the carriage. "I've been married for two minutes, and you're already trying to seduce my wife?"

I sucked in a sharp breath. *My wife*. Ruthless gods, that was what I was now. His wife.

"Can you blame me?" Rook replied with a slow grin, teeth flashing pearly white against his dark skin. Ugh, he was handsome. And he knew it.

I jumped at a distant explosion. Fuck, I needed to calm down. I was used to violence, but something on that scale ... it made me jumpy and scared. Genuinely scared.

The reality of war smacked me around the face. I thought I'd known what it was like, but nothing had prepared me for the ground shaking, for the sheer noise, or for the panic that gripped my chest.

Natasya had fought in the war, had lived with this fear day after day. Until the monster beside me shredded her to ribbons.

"What's your name?" the woman asked me abruptly, flipping her long blonde hair over her shoulder. She was dressed in full leather that made me miss my own leathers, stashed in a box in the back of the dressmaker's shop.

"Zabaletta," I replied quietly. Any louder, and my rage would come through, loud and clear.

"Pretty name," she remarked, sitting back in her seat to watch me. Assessing me, predator to prey. At least I looked pitiful enough to pass as a non-threat. I could thank the explosions for that, and the burning memory of Kier's grip on my wrist. My skin still crawled, like a dozen bee stings.

I gripped the padded bench under me when the carriage rocked over a pothole, gritting my teeth when it knocked me closer to Kier.

"Forgive me for noticing," Rook purred, "but you don't seem terribly happy to be married."

I swallowed. My answer had to be careful, clever, and not rouse suspicion. No pressure.

"All my life, I've heard stories of goblins' violence and cruelty. Would you be happy to marry someone like that?"

Kier stiffened, but let out a low, barely audible laugh. Bastard.

"Then why?" the woman—Xiona, he'd called her back at our wedding. Shee-ohn-a. "Why come forward at the tower?"

I swallowed down all my words except the ones that burned hotter, fiercer, than all the rest. "I lost my sister in the war."

"There you go, Kier," Xiona said, waving a hand at her silent friend. "Something for the two of you to bond over."

His answering snarl was so loud and sudden that I

recoiled into the carriage door, my heart in my throat and my wrist snapping to dislodge the tiny dagger up my sleeve. I caught it in my palm, keeping it hidden in the tulle and silk flowers of my skirts.

"You lost your sister, too?" I asked tightly, rage escaping into my voice.

Kier glanced my way, equally furious. He nodded. Said nothing.

"Where are we going?" I pressed while I was brave enough to talk.

"My home," he replied tersely, and the carriage fell into taut silence that no one apparently dared to break.

I curled my fingers around my knife and stared out the windows at the wind-blasted, barren lands rolling past, carrying me further than I'd ever been before.

No one spoke again for hours.

9

I had so many questions, but I didn't voice any of them as the carriage rolled far from the wastelands of the war zone and up a winding, rocky path between snow-capped mountains. I'd never been so far from home, or so far from humanity. I knew there were humans in the goblin lands, few though they were, but I felt like the first human to ever come this far west.

Xiona and Rook chatted amongst themselves, ignoring the heavy atmosphere on this side of the carriage. I didn't join in on their conversation, partly because seeming overwhelmed and quiet fit my role, but partly because I was nervous. I'd never been more aware of my mortality, of how quickly it could be snatched away. My fingers had locked painfully around the small knife hidden in the soft folds of my skirt, and I refused to let go. It was my safety blanket right now.

"Peasant," Rook said, laying a brightly painted card on the bench between him and Xiona with a languid flourish. The longer the journey had gone on, the more slumped he'd become. If we didn't reach the prince's home soon, he'd become horizontal.

Xiona's teeth flashed pearly white—her canines were sharp, but there were none of the needle teeth I'd heard goblins possessed. Not in this form, anyway. In her true form, she was probably horrific. "Merchant," she said smugly, laying a card on top of Rook's.

"I was hoping you'd say that," he purred. He did that a lot —softened his voice to a carnal caress. It made my skin itch and my heart rate pick up. I didn't like finding out that goblins had personalities like humans. I preferred to think of them all as empty-brained Neanderthals whose vocabulary consisted solely of *smash*, *destroy*, and *pillage*. "Noble."

"Fucker," Xiona spat, throwing the rest of her cards at him with a vicious flick of her wrist.

I watched them warily from the corner of my eye. I didn't know the game they were playing; it was nothing we played in Seagrave.

"I take it you don't have a royal," Rook said sweetly. "Sucks to be you, sweet Xiona."

"I'll pluck your eyes out while you sleep," Xiona hissed, startling a rough laugh from me.

I pretended not to notice their eyes slide to me, watching the bend in the road ahead, the mountains grey and rocky all around us. The further west we travelled, the colder it got, and a fog rolled in around the wheels of the carriage. My hateful companions never stopped to rest the horses or speak to the driver; on and on we rattled down the road. It had been *hours* since we'd left Merikand, and the sun was beginning to set already.

"You'd have to climb in bed with me to take my eyes," Rook pointed out, a smile in his voice. From the corner of my eye, I watched him slide a hand down his muscular chest. "You want some of this, Lilivatan?"

Xiona made a disgusted sound in the back of the throat. "I want your body as much as I want a swamp dog to feast on my bones."

Lilivatan—that had to be her surname. Xiona Lilivatan. I tucked the name away; it could come in handy.

I contemplated how I'd handle arriving at the prince's home when we finally reached it, running through a script in my head and absently watching the tendrils of fog creep in from the distance.

Xiona and Rook finally stopped bickering, the former leaning her head against the padded seat behind her and, to all intents and purposes, napping. I didn't buy that she was sleeping for a damn minute.

In the quiet, I decided to fish for information about the rebels. The explosions had shaken me; I wanted to know what kind of reception we could expect when we finally arrived at Kier's home. Would there be goblins with bombs and explosives waiting for us at this end?

"You said the attack at the tower was by rebels?" I asked quietly, casting a look vaguely in the direction of my monstrous husband.

Kier nodded his dark head, his mouth set in a harsh line and his eyes narrowing—anger lived there, deep set and endless. I knew the feeling; looking at him made my heart thunder in my chest.

"People who don't want peace, on either side," he explained, not casting me even a single look. Fine by me; I didn't want his vile eyes on me anyway. "They're a nuisance more than a real threat."

"The explosions felt real enough to me," I replied, unable

to keep the steel from my tone. "Aren't you worried one of them will get too close? They could kill you."

Xiona's eyes slitted open, watchful.

"I don't want to become a widow so young," I added, clenching the knife in my skirt and wanting to throw it into my husband's heart. Xiona and Rook would retaliate, though. I could fight three humans, especially with Rook so languorous and non-threatening, but three goblins?

It would come down to who was willing to fight the dirtiest, who was willing to put silly things like morals and conscience aside and do whatever it took to win.

"You won't become a widow," Kier replied with a scoff. "I'm a royal."

At my blank look, sensual Rook took pity on me and explained, "Goblin royals are almost a different breed; they have more power than the rest of us—"

"*A lot* more power," Xiona drawled.

My stomach sank. If goblin royals were immortal...

I'd failed Natasya.

"They live longer," Rook continued, watching me lazily. "And they're almost impossible to kill, except for one night a year."

"Should we be telling her this?" Xiona asked wryly. "She could use it against us. You know how bloodthirsty humans are."

"*Humans?*" I demanded, galled. "You're the ones slaughtering us—and for nothing!"

"Likewise, sweetheart," Xiona replied, her smile edged with venom. "I told you this was a bad idea, Kier," she snarled at him, her amber eyes piercing him as well as any sword.

I glanced at the prince in time to see him shoot a

quelling look at his friends. He was definitely the leader of this little group, then.

"You know as well as I do, this was our only option," he said quietly, probably hoping I wouldn't hear.

Louder, he added, "And I'm not worried about a little human killing me, even if she *is* smart enough to wait for the goblin moon when I'm vulnerable."

This little human eagerly tucked away that information. He was killable. I could still make him pay for what he'd done to my sister. But *wait*...?

How long would I have to wait until this moon showed up? A week? A month? Oh gods, what if there was only one every ten years?

My stomach knotted, grief's bruise spreading further across my heart.

Rook said, "She doesn't look particularly ferocious, Kier, I think you're safe."

It took every bit of effort and determination I had not to let the wolf in me shine through.

Let Kier sleep safely in his bed. Our bed—ugh. Let him be comfortable and complacent. If I had to wait, I had to wait. He was still dead when the goblin moon rose.

I didn't let myself think about all the things I'd need to do between now and the moon. Whatever it took—that's what I'd do.

I schooled my face into something nervous and pale, turning back to the window—and jolting at the sight of white, twisting fog all around us. I caught my breath at the flash of something silver through the creeping tendrils, like lightning but brighter.

"What the hell is that?" I gasped, my heart beating fast. I'd never seen fog move like that, never seen the scythe-like magic flashing within it.

Xiona shoved me aside and pressed her face against the window. "Gaia's tits," she swore, throwing a spearing look at Kier and then Rook. "The Haar," she snarled.

"The Haar?" I echoed, my heart rate picking up, enough that I realised it had settled since our frantic flight from the tower. That was unsettling in itself—these people were my enemy. Just because they weren't slaughtering humans now didn't mean they wouldn't be soon,

"Kinda hard to explain, brideling," Rook said, fishing a vial the size of his finger from the pocket of his sleeveless jacket and thumbing the stopper from it.

"It looks like fog," I said, peering out the window as the opaque white smoke swept in around the carriage's wheels. "But it's not." It wasn't a question, not really. But I wanted answers, and right the hell now.

Azure light splashed across the carriage floor—Kier twisted a ring around his tanned finger, the octagon-cut sapphire flashing with power.

"What the hell *is* that thing out there?" I demanded, too afraid to remember to be sweet. Fuck being sweet; even Orchid would be freaked out enough to swear right now.

"Magic," Kier responded grimly. "Stay in the carriage," he ordered, giving me a stern look as we came to an abrupt, jerking stop that sent me flying off the padded bench.

I landed on the floor in a heap of tulle. Not my finest moment. "Ow," I grunted, pain flashing up my tailbone.

My dear husband ignored my sound of pain, stepping heartlessly over the twisted train of my dress to throw the glossy carriage door open.

"Xio, stay with my wife," Kier ordered, leaping to the ground.

Xiona made a rough sound of complaint. "Why me? Rook can babysit her."

"I can babysit myself," I put in with a frown. No push-back on staying in the carriage though—if the fog was magic, I was staying as far away as possible.

"*Rook* has fog's ruin," Rook said with a quicksilver smile. He patted his friend on the shoulder as he followed Kier out of the carriage. "Try not to be mean," he added before he slammed the door and vanished around the front of the carriage.

Xiona made a disgusted face at the mere idea of niceties. Yeah, same.

"What kind of magic is the Haar?" I asked, watchful eyes on the twisting, creeping fog outside the window. Not that I knew a single thing about magic, and certainly not enough to know the difference between types. But if all I could arm myself with was information right now, I wanted as much of it as possible.

"Wild magic," Xiona muttered, sounding pissed off about having to answer me. "The kind that can't be controlled or harnessed or stopped."

I swallowed, my palm growing slick around my hidden dagger. "If it can't be stopped, how are we getting out of this?"

"It can be bribed," Xiona answered, her mouth twisted. She took out a dagger—prettier than mine, with thorns and roses cast in the metalwork of the handle—and began flipping it in her hand, end over end, hilt to blade to hilt. It never cut her once.

"Bribed by what?" I pressed.

"You're awfully curious." Her smile was as sharp as any weapon.

I laughed, letting all my bitterness about having to wait to kill Kier bleed through. "I'm in a land I don't understand, surrounded by strangers, and *now* there's a magic fog that could do gods know what to me—so *yes,* I'm curious. I don't want to die, thank you very much."

Xiona released a low, gruff laugh. "Fair point. It can be bribed by a mix of sugar and silversweet."

I blinked. That was *not* the answer I'd expected. I was braced for her to say dragon bones, a firebird feather, and the blood of a dozen virgins. Not silversweet—a leaf found in the mountains that cut the continent like a swath of broken teeth, separating goblin lands in the west and Lucre in the east. Silversweet looked like a sprig of mint, but distilled into a syrup it had calming properties that could soothe a raging bull.

Fog's ruin—that's what Rook said he had in that vial. I'd assumed it was poison, something cruel and clever. Not bloody *syrup.*

But if that was all it took to make the fog docile, I'd find a silversweet plant the first chance I got.

"Thanks," I forced myself to say. Orchid would definitely thank Xiona for the information.

She grunted a wordless reply, flicking her long, honey-blonde hair over her shoulder.

"What happens if we don't bribe it?" I asked, chewing the inside of my lip.

Xiona's expression darkened. "Nothing good. Anyone caught by it is found stripped bare."

"It takes their clothes?" I asked, frowning. Kinky.

"It devours their skin, their hair, their organs, even their bone marrow. Leaves only an empty skeleton for us to find."

Shit.

"Yeah," she agreed, seeing my expression.

Kier and Rook returned minutes later, the carriage sinking with their weight. Rook winked, confidence and ease written across his tall, sculpted body. Kier brooded, hunched and venomous, and sank onto the bench beside me so heavily that the carriage jumped on its wheels.

"The fog's gone?" I asked, peering out the window.

It had dissipated enough for me to see the mountains beside us again, the path disappearing around a bend. I breathed slightly easier now the fog had faded.

"It's gone, brideling," Rook confirmed cheerfully. Why did *he* have the fog's ruin, and not Kier? Surely their ringleader should be the one with the vial?

Weird, but not as troubling as their response when I asked, "And the driver's alright? They must have been surrounded by fog by the time you went out."

Xiona snorted. Kier laughed under his breath, a scornful rolling sound. Rook gave me a sad, pitying look that made my face splash with heat and my eyes narrow. I *hated* pity; it made me stabby.

"There's no driver," I guessed tightly, refusing to let my embarrassment show. "It's magic."

"Now you're getting it," Xiona remarked, amusement curling her upper lip off her teeth. "Don't worry, I'm sure you'll catch up soon enough."

It wasn't reassuring; it was a taunt.

It took every bit of my will power not to launch myself across the carriage and cross blades with her. I flexed my hand on the knife in my skirts, but if I attacked her, they'd reassess me. I'd be marked as dangerous, a threat—and any chance I had of killing my dear, sweet husband would be ruined.

He couldn't be killed except on the mysterious fucking goblin moon—but could he be weakened by the Haar? It was worth a shot, I decided.

I flattened the smile that wanted to cross my face, glancing out the window at the mountains again, and startling when we rounded a bend in the rocky path and a flat plain of grass and cornflower-blue flowers spread out in front of us.

A towering city squatted in the distance, made of grey brick with sapphire rooftops, and a fairy-tale castle rose higher than all the other buildings with conical towers, shining cobalt windows, and flags waving in a frantic wind.

It was a fitting home for a prince, but too damn pretty for a goblin.

"Finally," Xiona groaned, putting away her knife.

Rook flashed me a smile and said what my husband should have. "Welcome to Lazankh, City of Sapphires, Zabaletta."

10

*T*he City of Sapphires was too pretty a name for a damn goblin city. This place was too pretty for goblins, full stop. Hand-painted glass shone azure and sky and ice blue, pale grey brick gleaming in the sunset light. Everything that could be accented blue was; the city more than lived up to its name.

"I take it you live in the castle," I said as we drove up a broad avenue made from the same grey stone as the buildings.

People stopped their errands to watch the carriage roll past, murmuring to their friends or children about us. Did they know their prince had married a human? Did they know about the fog that was eating people to their bones?

I slipped my knife back into its sheath and clenched my hands into fists, hidden by the voluminous tulle of my skirts, as I spotted blue-skinned goblins among the gawking people. Some had pale, golden, and brown skin like humans, but a lot of them were as blue as the ocean, or as icy as a frozen lake, or as deep-skinned as a night sky. Claws, horns, tusks, and razor teeth were everywhere I looked. My breathing sped.

Natasya's shredded body flashed in my mind, and my relentless need for vengeance was swamped by fear for my own life. What the hell was I doing here? What was I *thinking?*

"You're their princess," Kier said in a gravel-rough voice, his eyes narrowed as he watched me. "Don't insult your people by being scared of them."

"My sister was *slaughtered* by one of them," I snapped, unable to stop a glare forming.

"My sister was murdered by one of you," he replied coldly, blue-black eyes flashing.

"Eek," Rook said out the side of his mouth to Xiona.

"And they're supposed to be in the honeymoon period," she drawled back.

"This isn't a fucking joke," I snarled at them, unable to soften myself, to pull back the spiral of panic and primal fear. "People died. People are *still* dying—and even with this bullshit marriage, people will continue to die."

Kier shocked me by nodding, black hair tumbling around his face.

But he asked me, "If you don't think the marriage will end the war, why bother getting married to me?"

I dragged a breath through my nose, forcing myself to think straight. "I had to try something," I said finally, my anger calming but my terror not budging a damn inch.

Once I killed him, I'd have to sneak out of a castle full of goblins, navigate a city brimming with even more, and then cross their twisted, magic-wracked land. I'd been so rash, so thoughtless, when I rushed to the tower to get married. I'd been so blinded by excitement at finally killing him that I hadn't considered myself—how much danger I'd be in. How hard it would be to get out.

I hadn't contemplated that goblins would have cities and civilisation for fuck's sake. I was out of my depth.

Kier was still watching me, a deeply unsettled look on his tanned face. "So did I," he said finally. "I had to try something."

He blew out a hard breath, sounding like a person and not a monster. It was unsettling as fuck. "Nothing else had slowed this war, let alone stopped it. At least our wedding had a chance of bringing a temporary ceasefire. With any luck, it'll hold for months."

Xiona made a sound of agreement, her attention on the city outside the window, gleaming and beautiful even with some buildings in dire need of roofs and shutters repaired. That neglect was the only sign this city belonged to a warring country; there were no tumbledown buildings, no wreckage, no hastily repaired shops like in Merikand.

Even if I would have to live among enemies and monsters, at least we were far enough from the war-front here to escape that ruin.

Unless the rebels followed us across the border, that was.

Gates of glimmering lapis carved with vines and leaves swung open when we reached the walled castle at the end of the road. A flurry of gold-liveried attendants and guards were already lined up at the maw of the castle to accept us. Nerves twisted my stomach; I would be surrounded, hemmed in on all sides by goblins who'd tear me to shreds if they discovered the truth of why I was here. Or maybe they'd do that anyway just for fun.

"Before we go inside," my monstrous husband said, twisting towards me and making my skin prickle at the attention. "Don't leave the castle until I've announced our marriage and you've been presented to the people. There are some goblins who aren't as tolerant of your kind as we are."

"Pigs," Xiona spat, making me blink. I hadn't pegged her as someone who'd be sympathetic to humans. Surely she hated us as much as we hated her? "Don't get it twisted," she laughed, seeing my attention. "I hate humans as much as the next goblin. You cruel fucks tortured my best friend. I had to blow apart a whole fortress to get him—"

"Xio," Rook growled through gritted teeth, his face taut with anger. "Tell your own fucking story if you want to get chatty."

I kept my expression as neutral as possible. And here I'd been thinking Rook was harmless—but he'd withstood torture and lived to see another day? He had as much cause to hate me as I did to hate him. He might not have killed Natasya, but he was best buds with the man who had. And I might not have tortured him, but if it served me, I would have.

I couldn't underestimate the lazy, flirtatious man.

Xiona fleetingly set her hand on Rook's knee, so fast I could have imagined it, but there was no hiding the glance of forgiveness he shot her way. Best friend, she'd called him. They were a unit—close-knit and loyal. If they were the same with Kier, that would make getting out after I took my revenge infinitely harder. Fuck, this was going to be impossible.

Part of me wanted to jump out of the carriage and run all the way back to the mortal lands. But one look at the guards lined up at the castle steps, clad in gold and each holding a staff tipped with sapphires the size of a hen's egg

—bigger even than the one Kier wore on his lapel—and I knew getting out would be nowhere near as easy as sneaking out of Celandrine's barracks. Damn near impossible, in fact.

I had to bide my time, bite my tongue, and find a way to sneak out. Every security system had a weakness; I just had to discover theirs.

I jumped when the carriage door opened, a footman with icy skin and midnight-blue eyebrows, hair, and lips sweeping it back for us to exit.

"Pretend to like me," Kier said, a second before he grabbed my hand. Thank fuck I'd put my knife away; that would have been awkward to explain.

I had half a second to scramble my brain around that order before he was tugging me off the bench and guiding me out of the carriage. Eyes burned my skin from all directions, and I tensed.

"This is gonna be good, I can sense it," Xiona said with a slashed grin as he jumped down after us, a dozen knives, swords, and fuck knows what else rattling on her body.

"It'll be fine," Kier said tightly, shooting her a look that clearly said *shut the fuck up*. If the footman heard the exchange, he didn't let on.

I stayed quiet, calculating my move as Kier guided me across the mosaic floor of the courtyard towards the arrayed staff. Voices from behind made my hackles raise, and I twisted to protect my back.

People pressed against the great lapis gates, faces crammed between the twisting, organic designs, eyes hungry. I faced forward again, my stomach flipping.

"They've come for a glimpse of the new princess," Rook said with a slow smile.

So everyone knew about the wedding here, too. Great.

I focused on the tiles beneath my feet—a swirling design of clouds and blue leaves that came together to form a face—instead of dwelling on the fact I was a fucking *princess*. That hadn't occurred to me when I'd raced across Lucre to marry a beast.

A princess. Of a fucking goblin kingdom. With subjects, and people, and duties.

"I want to introduce you before anyone else meets her," Kier said to the staff, his voice rich with authority and stateliness.

They watched us with bright, curious eyes. Not as greedy as the people at the gate, but still staring at me like I was a jade vase in a glass gallery case.

"This is my wife," Kier said with great ceremony, sweeping a hand at me.

I suppressed a smirk when I realised he needed me to finish his introduction. He didn't remember my name. I was glad our wedding had been *so* memorable for him.

I was getting the sense I was an obligation, something he'd put up with to stop the war, at least for a while. Which was fine by me; if he didn't want a wife, he'd be less inclined to monitor my comings and goings.

Stay in the castle until he'd introduced me? Ha, as if!

"Zabaletta Stellara," I announced, forcing myself to meet their gazes, as if I was a real princess, benevolent and caring. I'd kill any one of these people if they stood between me and my revenge, but I hid all that behind a neutral mask.

"Kollastus," Kier corrected, squeezing my hand in warning. I squeezed it right back, hard enough to grind his fingers, and he straightened his spine.

Oops, I shouldn't have done that. Orchid wouldn't have done that. I eased up my grip.

"Zabaletta Kollastus," I said to the gathered staff, pasting on a smile that was damn good, even if I did say so myself. "I know this is unconventional, but I want to make the best of my new life here. I don't want to be your enemy."

I was channelling Orchid hard, but heads tilted with interest, buying the shit I was peddling. My hand itched, the press of Kier's skin against mine abhorrent.

"Humans are welcome here, your highness," a tall woman with light brown skin and freckles said, ignoring the warning glance a scary, blue-haired woman shot at her. "You'll be safe with us."

I blinked, not faking my surprise. She'd gone out of her way to reassure me, and risked pissing off her superior. For a stranger—and a human?

"I'm a halfling," she added with a pretty smile.

"Calanthe," the sour-faced superior ground out. "I'm sorry, your highnesses," she added, curtsying deep. "My maid is prone to bursts of outspokenness, it's the—"

She cut herself off, leaving an awkward pause.

"The human in her?" I guessed wryly, wondering if I could extricate my hand without causing a scene. Kier's touch was in-fucking-tolerable.

Humans might have been accepted here, but there were clearly insidious prejudices that weren't leaving any time soon. I doubted Sour Face even gave a second thought to her comment until it was halfway out of her pursed mouth.

I shrugged, probably too casually for a princess. Ah, well. "Don't worry, I won't hold it against you," I assured the woman, and watched her swallow the need to thank me with the same sourness as a lemon.

She curtsied. "Many thanks, your highness."

Kier, clearly done here, tugged on my hand, sending a shudder of revulsion through my body that I knew full well he felt. "Have dinner brought to my private hall tonight," he ordered, but absent the vicious entitlement I'd expected.

His staff bowed, some hurrying off to make his dinner. I pasted a bland look of curiosity on my face as he led me up the wide, blue steps and into his home.

It felt like walking into the mouth of a hungry shark.

11

Please don't go, I wanted to beg Xiona and Rook as they clapped the goblin prince on the shoulder, gave me a wary nod—Xiona—and a wink—Rook—and then went their separate ways.

Leaving me alone with my new husband.

There were no staff this deep in the castle, although someone had to turn up soon to deliver the dinner Kier had ordered. I walked stiffly beside him down a corridor every bit as graceful and beautiful as the outside of the castle. The walls were bare, silvery brick, but everything else was a shade of blue, so much that curiosity bit at me and I spoke.

"What's with all the blue?" I asked, slanting a look at my hateful husband as he led me into an interior courtyard, a blue glass dome hanging overhead and a pale balustrade ringing the mezzanine above. In the middle of the space, padded chairs were arranged around a low table. It looked like somewhere people would lounge around getting trashed after work, and I could *not* picture goblins there, with their blue skin and tusks and horns, beers in hand.

"There are two goblin courts," Kier replied, watching me

the same way I watched him—from the corner of his eye, with barely-hidden displeasure. "Bluescale and Greenheart."

"Huh," I said, trailing my gaze over our surroundings as he aimed for a pale staircase to the mezzanine level. I marked six exits, and committed them to memory. "So Bluescale then?"

Kier nodded. Said nothing. Right, then. If I wanted to mine anyone for information, it would have to be someone else. Maybe I could find the pretty, half-human maid.

"These are my rooms, no one else can come here," he explained, aiming for an archway off the upper level. After a pause, he corrected, "Our rooms. If you want to invite anyone here, you'll have to run it by me first, and I'll do the same. Rook and Xiona are free to come and go as they please, and my staff too."

"Our staff," I said sweetly, earning an irritated glare. I calmed myself by picturing the way his eyeballs would burst when I stabbed them.

"Our staff," he agreed through gritted teeth. And then with some relief, "Here's the dining room. Eat whatever you want."

He strode through an open archway into a small but opulent hall dominated by a polished marble table. For a second I just stared at the excessive amount of food covering it—plates and bowls, tureens and platters, all full of fresh food. No way had the staff made all this in the little time they'd had.

"This is magic, isn't it?" I asked suspiciously, eyeing a spiral of bread as if it would grow legs and perform a can-can. Hell, maybe it would.

"Not the food itself, only the process used to make it," he explained, piling meat onto a plate and ignoring the vegetables. Good to know men were the same across species.

"What kind of process?" I asked, poking the bread and honestly surprised when it didn't shout in complaint.

"Instead of an oven, magic can be used to cook something in a few seconds. The same for mixing, chopping, and everything else that goes into making food."

"A prince like you wouldn't know how to cook," I guessed, barely covering the acid in my voice.

"And I suppose you're from a common family who slaved over an oven day and night?" he returned, watching me from across the table.

I tried not to look at him full-on. His normal appearance was unsettling.

"If that's what you'd like to think," I replied, examining a tureen of soup. Little pastry things floated in it; I narrowed my eyes at them.

Kier snorted.

I snapped my head up and found him watching me with a smirk.

"*What?*" I demanded, and swore at myself for not softening my words. I needed him to believe I was harmless, not prone to fits of temper. Even if I was—and struggled to hide it even on my best days.

"You've never seen dumpling soup before?" he asked with a low rumble of laughter.

I *just* managed to stop myself giving him the middle finger, but there was no hiding my scowl.

"It won't bite," he said, still laughing at me as he headed for the door. "Try it."

"Don't you think that's a little insensitive," I bit out, my temper even hotter, "given how many throats you people have ripped out?"

I went still as he came around the table, his body language changing between one step and the next. A predator stalked towards me, and I was unaccustomed to being prey. It was a sickly feeling. I hated it.

"And yet you'd use a knife despite how many goblin hearts you people have carved out," he returned tightly, advancing towards me with his plate in his hand. Good. I could knock it into his face and run if it came to it.

I'll carve out your heart too, dear husband, I thought. I wanted to say it to his face so badly.

"Enjoy your night," he threw at me, and stalked out the door.

"Hey, what the hell! You can't just leave me here. Where am I supposed to sleep?"

"Find a room," he called from the hallway, ignoring me when I burst out the archway and glared daggers at the back of his head. I could kill him right now, throw a knife right into his skull—except I couldn't. The bastard wouldn't die.

I growled and stormed back into the dining room. If I had to endure this place for fuck knows how long, at least I could do it on a full stomach.

When I'd eaten, I picked the biggest room I could find just to spite my husband. It probably had some fancy name, but I couldn't give two shits. It had double glass doors and a balcony that would make a perfect escape route, a heavy lock on the door, and wooden beams crisscrossing the ceiling that would be easy enough to hide amongst if I needed to. It was amazing how few people looked up when searching a room.

"Home sweet home," I sighed, flopping onto the bed and groaning as the mattress hugged my body. I'd been tense all day, and now I ached like crazy.

At least with the door locked, I could let all the pretence and bullshit fall away. I expelled a slow breath, rubbing my face. I didn't even try to sleep; I knew I wouldn't be able to rest in this castle, with goblins streaming around downstairs. With Kier Kollastus somewhere close by.

How long until the goblin moon? How long would I have to endure this hell?

I got up and dragged the seafoam wedding dress over my head, leaving it in a puddle on the floor as I explored the wardrobes and drawers—empty. Great. I stayed in the white shift, removing most of my weapons so I could lay comfortably, but keeping the strap around my forearm. I refused to be completely defenceless, even while relaxing.

What was Kier doing right now? Was he already sleeping soundly, his conscience clear despite all the horrors he'd committed? Was he entertaining a lover, despite his new wife? The thought pissed me off on behalf of an imaginary real bride. Orchid deserved better. Fuck that, *I* deserved better. I came here to kill him, but he didn't know that.

He'd been a dick all day, and if I hadn't had revenge to keep me going, that might have affected me. He'd scowled and sneered and laughed like I was dirt, when as far as he knew, I'd married him for the same reason he'd married me: for peace, however temporary.

Clearly, he didn't plan to treat me like a real wife. Which suited me fine. Anything to make plotting his murder easier.

First things first, I needed to know when the goblin moon fell. And find where he slept.

I ignored the stare of the haunted woman in the tall, brass mirror opposite the bed—my own stare—and closed my eyes.

I didn't know what would happen tomorrow, but at least I'd had a meal. At least I wasn't hungry anymore.

a cockerel screamed, startling me from a drowsy half-sleep, and I swore viciously. I shot upright, dagger in my hand, half tempted to throw it at the offending animal if it didn't shut the hell up. Instead, I hauled myself out of bed and glared across the cobalt rooftops, spotting the loud bastard after a minute. I didn't throw my dagger—I was a criminal and assassin, not a monster—but I pointed it threateningly at the beast when he tilted his head back for another deafening bellow.

"Arsehole," I muttered when he screamed again. There was no need for it.

Escaping these alarm calls should have been the one positive thing to coming to the goblin lands, but *of course* this hell had roosters, too. I swore the fucker turned and looked at me, as if he could sense my irritation, but he was probably looking at the flags I could hear flapping on the towers above.

I had no idea where this room was in relation to the rest of the castle; that would be my job for today. Learn the layout of the castle, and subtly inquire about the goblin moon's date.

Footsteps scraped outside my door, and I drew my arm back, knife poised to fly—before I remembered the role I was supposed to play, and hid the dagger behind the long curtains I hadn't bothered to shut last night. I unfastened the strap on my forearm in a panic, stuffing it behind the blue curtain just as the door opened.

The beautiful, brown-skinned woman from yesterday burst through the door, the tray in her hands bearing both a plate full of breakfast and—*oh, thank the gods*—underwear, hygiene products, and a hair brush. I didn't consider myself vain, but brushing my hair and having clean underwear were luxuries I was accustomed to.

I wasn't here to make friends, but something drew me to this woman. Maybe because she was the only human I'd seen since entering this gods-forsaken place. Maybe because of her infectious smile. Her eyes crinkled as she aimed that disarming grin my way.

"You just became my new favourite person," I said, not having to fake my smile.

"For the sweetcakes or the underwear?" she asked with a trilling laugh that, honest to gods, sounded like birdsong. I'd always thought that description was cliché and bullshit, but the maid's beauty was reflected in her voice.

"Both," I replied, moving from the window so she'd have no reason to find my hidden knife.

"Goblins get their cycle differently to humans, so I know what it's like. I don't know if you need these now, but at least you'll have them whenever you do."

Ugh, she was kind. And nice. And *sweet*. It was impossible to hate her.

"What's your name?" I asked, resigning myself to a new

friend. Yesterday Rook had adopted me as his friend/flirting recipient, but this was all on me.

What if pretending to be Orchid-like made me into someone like her? Sweet and wholesome, without hands stained with blood and nailbeds dirty from scaling walls to evade capture?

Ugh.

"Calanthe," the maid replied easily, not offended even though I should have remembered it from yesterday. A real princess would have remembered. Good thing I was just a fake.

But then Calanthe set her tray on a carved wooden table against the wall and said, "Your presentation is later this afternoon. Are you excited?"

I couldn't hide my true reaction quick enough. Calanthe's whole face softened, her brown-hazel eyes literally sparkling with sympathy. She looked like a painting from one of the great artists of the first age come to life. I wouldn't be surprised if stars started shining in a halo around her head, or golden rays of sun shone from her bushy curls.

"Nervous?" she amended with a wince.

Yeah, let's go with that. Not disgusted, terrified, and so far out of my depth I was off the ground and into the sky. Me, who hated every single goblin who walked the earth— fucking *princess* of them.

"Definitely," I agreed. "I don't know what to expect," I added, hoping I sounded pitiful. "I don't know anything about goblins, or their royals, or *any* of this." I flung my arms out at the room.

"If there's a prince, there has to be a king, right?" I knew there was because there were stories of his idleness and arrogance, but he never stepped foot on the battlefields unlike his sons. He never led the armies or crushed human towns or murdered my sister. But maybe he was worse. Maybe they held him back because even goblins wouldn't be safe near him. "Will he be at my announcement?"

Calanthe touched my shoulder before she remembered our wildly differing status and dropped her hand with a grimace. "Don't worry, the king stays in Skayan."

At my blank look, she rushed to add, "That's the capital of the Bluescale court, where the king and most of the royals live. It's ... not like Lazankh."

I snagged a berry from the breakfast plate and chewed, surprised at the sweetness. Were these grown with magic? Actually, I didn't want to know.

"They're not tolerant of humans," I guessed.

"Not at all," she laughed, trying to play it off. "Even halflings like me are made to feel unwelcome there. But I hear the mountains are beautiful," she rushed to add. "And the palace is built right into the side of the biggest one, part of the rock itself. The floors are said to be carpeted with petals and there's a curtain of pure blue roses behind the throne."

"Sounds lovely," I murmured, folding a sweetcake in half and devouring it whole. I ignored the wide-eyed look Calanthe gave me, throwing a few more berries down my gullet. Gods, I was starving. I'd eaten last night, but before that ... nothing all day. Not since the fresh bread roll I'd slid from a baker's windowsill before dawn.

"Not as lovely as Lazankh," she whispered, as if someone would hear and report her words back to the capital. "These streets are my favourite."

My ears pricked. So she knew the city well. "Maybe you can give me a tour," I suggested. "I should get to know the city if I'm going to be the princess of it. Meet some of the locals, you know."

Calanthe beamed, downright delighted. "It would be my honour. I'll have to clear it with Dove."

"Dove?" I frowned, helping myself to the rest of my breakfast. I knew I was eating like a street urchin, but some habits were impossible to break once you'd learned them. When Uncle Tavish kicked us out, we'd had to find food wherever we could, and it was always scarce. Still, nothing could convince me to eat that dumpling soup from the table last night. Little floating things in a soup? Unnatural.

"The castle matron," Calanthe explained, folding my new underwear into a drawer. How had she found me? I could have chosen any room in the castle...

"That battle axe is called *Dove?*" I blurted, laughter cracking out of me. Damn.

Calanthe shot me a grin. "I know. I thought the same thing when I first met her."

"Where were you before?" I asked, curious about my new maid. I hadn't had a maid in fucking years, but already Calanthe was better than the sour-faced woman I'd grown up with.

"Oh, my family lives in the mountains," she answered with a strained smile, turning to straighten my bed covers.

"The mountains," I echoed, my mind turning over. "Where a lot of the fighting is?"

Calanthe nodded without looking back. "It's a hard place to live, but it's home. My family's still there; we've been there for generations, and I can't see us budging any time soon."

"Then why work for the prince?" I asked, and wondered if I'd overstepped. If people pried too closely into my personal life, I convinced them to mind their own business at knifepoint. "You don't have to answer that," I added.

"It's fine," she replied with an eye-crinkling smile. Gods,

she was pretty. Did she even realise? "I came here chasing love." She laughed, self-deprecating as hell.

Now I was the one giving her soft-eyed looks. I shoved the last of the sweetcakes into my mouth, wondering how the goblin and human lands had so much in common. The batter of these had been spiced with something sweet and earthy, but I could easily have bought these from a stand near Seagrave's bay.

"It didn't work out, I take it," I said carefully. Few memories could hurt as brutally as heartbreak.

Calanthe waved a freckled hand, then set about fluffing up my pillows. "I confessed my love, and she laughed in my face. Said she'd never stoop to date someone with dirt in their blood."

I hissed in offence. "So that's what they call you—goblin and human children, I mean."

She nodded, her curls bouncing along her back. "Dirty. It's fine, I'm used to it."

It wasn't fine. And *I* certainly wouldn't get used to it if they called me the same. A real princess would probably handle it with dignity and grace. I'd handle it with a sharp tongue and sharper steel.

Speaking of ... Calanthe headed for the balcony curtains next, and I panicked, taking a rushed step forward.

"Oh, leave those," I said with a note of soft authority, wondering if my new princess status would allow me to issue commands without being questioned.

Please, please...

"I like the light the way it is," I added.

It sounded plausible. I mentally patted myself on the back for the cover story. Calanthe gave me a big smile and nodded, stepping away.

Thank fuck.

"Of course," she said, and then added with so much kindness, "You're a princess now. I know it must be strange, but you can have anything you want here."

Your prince's head served on a platter to his own horse.

Oh right, we didn't do horses here. We had *magic*. Fucking magic. If humans could get by without it, why did these people feel the need to put it in every damn thing? If even food wasn't sacred, what was?

"Definitely strange," I agreed. "I'm not a peasant like the prince seems to think, but no way am I used to this level of ... everything."

"It overwhelmed me, too, when I first came here," Calanthe said comfortingly, looking like she wanted to touch my arm as she came closer. "You'll get used to it, don't worry."

Oh, speaking of worries!

I bit my lip, casting my gaze to the rug at my feet. I hadn't even noticed it last night, but now I trailed my eyes over the blue dragon woven into its threads.

"Kier mentioned something yesterday," I said, sounding suitably worried, and strategically using his name so it sounded like I gave a shit about him. "He said he's in danger at the goblin moon." I lifted my eyes, giving her *new bride in a strange land afraid to be widowed* energy. "What if someone hurts him? Where will I go?"

"Oh, princess," Calanthe murmured, her eyes so big and sympathetic I actually felt a twinge of guilt. "It'll be okay. All the royals cloister themselves away during the goblin moon —the only person who'll be with him all day will be you."

Ooh!

I faked a ragged breath of relief. "So no one else can get in?"

"Even the servants aren't allowed into these rooms when it's the goblin moon," she promised.

Fuck, it'd be obvious I was the one who'd killed him. But if I could get far enough away before they discovered his body, it might work.

"And it's not for a month, so there's no need to trouble yourself," Calanthe added, reaching out and squeezing my hand.

I made sure to squeeze hers back, if only in thanks at the information she'd given me. We both jumped at a knock on the door, but Calanthe laughed and let go of me.

"That'll be the dressmaker. We need to get you looking beautiful for your announcement, don't we?"

She headed for the door, her gold uniform skirt swishing around her ankles—but she paused with her hand on the doorknob. "Don't let the worries win, okay? Things will be okay here, I promise. And the prince is a good man. You'll always be safe with him."

Safe with my sister's murderer? Yeah. Sounded likely.

"Just get through today's event," she added with one of those infectious smiles, "and tomorrow we can escape to explore the city. Dove won't say no if I tell her it was the princess's request."

Calanthe was invaluable. I gave her a smile and nodded, even if I kept turning her words over and over inside my mind.

It's not for a month.

A fucking *month.*

I'd been willing to do anything to get justice for Natasya's murder, but this ... spending a whole month with her murderer ... I didn't know if I could do it.

13

"Smile," Kier said out of the corner of his mouth, his hand raised in the fakest wave I'd seen in my life. And I'd watched Celandrine practise her benevolent waving for hours on end while her acolytes trained.

"*You* smile," I shot back. My patience was already worn down, and we'd been on this stage in the middle of a grey-stone courtyard for exactly two minutes.

"I *am* smiling," he ground out, though what twisted his lips was more of a snarl than a smile.

I smirked at his pitiful attempt. Huh, look at that. It was a miracle. I was smiling.

"Smirking doesn't count," he muttered.

"Aw, boo hoo," I hissed.

Orchid was nowhere to be seen today; there were too many people staring at me, screaming their heads off, manically waving blue flags, pressing up to the stage with their hands raised for a touch I'd rather die than give them.

Kier blinked at the acid dripping from my voice. I'd return to my sweet, beleaguered wife routine later; now I was just fighting through the next hour, counting down the minutes until we could leave.

"I can't smile on command," I added, but gave a half-hearted wave at a red-faced woman nearby and watched a genuine smile bloom on her face.

"Some princess you are," he muttered, waving at a little, blue-skinned kid as they were propped on their dad's brawny shoulders.

"Some husband you are," I threw back. "Comfort your overwhelmed wife, won't you?"

I said it to be cutting—to be a dick, honestly. If I was suffering, he should be too. But Kier blinked, and seemed to realise that I was genuinely uncomfortable with the screaming masses. He shuffled closer, as if *that* would be a comfort. But at least he stopped antagonising me; this was hard enough without trying to hold myself in check. With everyone staring at our stage, there was no way I could plunge a knife into his heart.

It was tempting, though, when he clasped my hand—and the crowd went fucking wild.

Weirdos.

The only other person on stage with us was a herald from the capital, decked out in ocean blue livery, down to his stockings and frilly shirt. He looked ridiculous. I badly wanted to tell him the cap on his head would look better at a jaunty angle. Every hat looked better at a jaunty angle.

When Kier and I had walked onto the stage, the herald had made a racket blowing a bugle and then boomed so everyone could hear, "His royal highness, Kier Kollastus, and his new bride, her royal highness, Zabaletta Kollastus."

I hated the name, but it was all part of the trial I had to endure to give Natasya the justice she deserved. I didn't want to know what she'd think, looking down on me standing beside her killer, but she'd be proud when I avenged her. I knew she would.

Now the herald stood watching us with as much curiosity, admiration, and awe as half the crowd. The rest hung back, watchful, measuring. Did they hate humans like Dove did—like the prince himself did? Or did they just think I was a weak princess because I was human? If only they knew all the blood on my hands, all the contracts I'd filled working as an assassin in rough Seagrave. Maybe they'd respect that; goblins were known for their own ruthlessness, after all.

"Princess!" a little kid screamed—a girl, maybe? It was hard to tell since she was as vivid as a blueberry, with a little tuft of black hair, and dressed in a bright yellow puffy coat. "Princess!"

She was just a kid. My stomach twisted. I hated her with all the passion in my shrivelled heart, and she was just a kid.

I waved at her, forcing my smirk into a smile, guilt corrosive in my belly.

"Shit," Kier hissed under his breath.

I shot him an alarmed look at the pure horror in his voice—the most emotive I'd heard since we met. "What? Rebels?"

"Worse," he grunted, his fingers flexing around my hand. I'd been trying to forget that our hands were clasped together, that his warm, dry palm was pressed to mine. If I dissociated with my hand, it wasn't really happening. "You can't hear that?"

I pricked my ears, on full alert. I knew he noticed, watched me go into survival mode, and I could do nothing to stop it.

But then I heard it, and I understood his reaction. *Shit* was a tame reaction. I was going to be sick.

A chant crawled from the middle of the crowd to the platform we waved from—*kiss, kiss, kiss!*

"We could run," I offered quietly, remembering to wave, to play the perfect princess.

"Ha! They'd chase after us."

"Gods."

Kier frowned in my vague direction. "Plural? Humans have more than one god?"

I frowned in *his* vague direction, shutting out the chants. "Of course we do. Goblins only have one?"

"Gaia, the Mother," he confirmed tightly, less at the religion discussion than the peer pressure from the crowd.

"We have the Sea, the Earth, and the Sky."

"Those are things," he argued, his fingers tighter around mine with every scream of *kiss! kiss!*

My smile became a wince; I squeezed his right back, hard enough to rearrange the bones in his hand, and he hissed. Point well made, I thought.

"To you they are. To humans, there's no such thing as the Mother."

He hissed in offence.

"Yeah, that's how I felt when you told me my gods are made-up. Feel good?"

"No."

"Same," I muttered, every slam of my heart against my ribs screaming *my sister's killer, my sister's killer, my sister's killer.*

The crowd yelled hysterically, urging me to kiss the man who'd shredded Natasya with his claws until she wasn't even recognisable.

"Let's just get this over with, and then we'll leave," Kier muttered.

A compromise. Stand here for another forty minutes—

or kiss him. I couldn't bear either. I swallowed hard, the air tasting different here—no salt, no brine, no metallic tang of welders building ships by the docks.

"Princess!" another kid shouted. I met his eyes, and hated myself for hating him. He'd done nothing to me, but I would happily raze his city to the ground. The guilt was impossible to swallow.

"Make it quick," I ground out to Kier. I needed to get away from this crowd, from their innocent, excitement-filled eyes that made me question everything I believed.

Kier didn't waste time; maybe he was as eager to get off this platform as I was. He tugged me hard so I slammed into his chest, and my hand flew up automatically to catch me. Velvet brocade brushed my palm, his outfit as elegant as mine. I wondered if he'd been forced to stand still while a glaring dress-maker gestured and sent fabrics flying magically through the air, moulding to my body with the flash of a sapphire pendant.

The crowd's noise became unbearable, their volume screeching higher as Kier ducked his head. There was nowhere else to look except at his hateful face bending over me. I hated the slant of his eyes and the sharp edges of his cheekbones and his brutal jaw, and especially the cruel lips that pressed against mine in a chaste kiss.

I shuddered, revulsion twisting my stomach even as a thrill zapped through my body like lightning burning a tree from the inside out. I hated that I didn't hate it at all, and wrenched back hard.

The crowd was riotous. Kier's eyes were pinched, shame filling them in a reflection of my own. I wasn't supposed to feel anything from that press of scowling mouths. I certainly wasn't supposed to feel heat and sparks. Neither, apparently, was he.

He recovered faster than me, aiming a wry smile at the crowd and raising his voice to be heard, impossibly, over the screaming. "Thank you for showing such a warm acceptance for my wife. Together, we'll usher in a time of peace for the Bluescale court. You have my word on this."

He nodded at a group of people dressed in leather-scaled uniforms who'd hung back from the stage, and they created a pathway for us to escape. Interesting that Kier had brought guards for our outing today when he hadn't felt the need for them at our wedding. Where rebels had blown the whole place up.

Clearly things weren't quite as rosy in Lazankh as they looked.

"Wait!" someone shouted as we descended the wooden platform steps, the voice clear and strong, followed by grunts of complaint. "Your highness! The Haar!"

Kier froze and snapped his head around, searching the crowd from halfway down the steps. I found the man before he did—ha, take that, you smug bastard!—and pointed him out to my dear, beloved husband.

The man was a frazzled-looking goblin with icy skin, glasses, and wayward hair. Dressed in tweed, he could have been any number of professors hired by my uncle who'd tried to manage my wild streak. If I ignored the blue skin, anyway.

"It races for the village of Cyana now."

"Shit," Kier swore viciously, straightening and looking every inch the goblin predator, capable of ripping apart a body, shredding the insides, and leaving them on the edge of a city for their sister to find. I took a careful step away, eyeing the black-scaled guards who'd no doubt grab me if I tried to run.

"We'll ride out now," he promised the man, and then rushed down the rest of the steps.

I followed, warily watching everything around me, waiting for an attack and ready to defend myself.

"Verify the rumour," Kier growled at one of his guards; she nodded and peeled away as the others closed in around us, making me instantly claustrophobic. I was trapped, hemmed in on all sides by my enemy, and on the other side of their oppressive black bodies were hundreds more who'd slaughter me.

"Zabaletta," Kier said quietly, making me jump with a hand on my arm.

I snapped the knife I'd hidden up my sleeve into my hand but caught myself before I could use it, surprised at the emotion pinching his eyes and mouth. Something like sadness, like understanding, like humanity. *Oh, fuck you.*

"My guards will take you back to the castle—"

Where I'd be kept locked up under armed guard? I didn't fucking think so.

"I'm coming with you," I argued, my heart beating fiercely. I didn't want to be near him for another second more, my lips still burning. Like I'd kissed a pool of lava and burned the skin off of them.

Before he could argue, I added, "Some princess I'd be if I let my people fight their battles alone."

Twisting his earlier words back on him. If I couldn't use steel, I could use another of my favourite weapons—clever words.

"Fine," he spat, his tanned face twisted with displeasure. "But you stay with me—you don't budge an inch from my side."

"Or what?" I laughed quietly. "You'll lose your wife to the fog? I'm sure you'd be devastated."

"I married you to end the fucking war," he snarled, teeth bared and sending a flash of primal fear through me. "Getting you killed would only launch it twice as violently."

"Then why risk bringing me along?" I asked, even though I should have kept my mouth shut. He was going along with what I wanted for gods' sakes.

The look Kier sent my way was so scathing it could have cut me. "I'm your husband, not your owner. I won't tell you what you can't do."

Huh. That was inconveniently admirable.

Disquiet crept into my heart like the white fog of the Haar as the guards led us through the crowd to the carriage —not to take us to the castle, but to spirit us into danger. To rescue a goblin village.

What the fuck was I thinking?

14

"*T*his place is a mess," I said to myself as the carriage glided down a winding slope cut into a rolling hill—blue, of course, instead of green. I was getting the sense the Bluescale court wasn't so fond of Greenheart, going so far as to plant blue flowers to cover up the grass.

The village was visible at the base of the hill, part of it swallowed by a thick, white fog, but the rest in ruins, all buildings crumbled, roofs eaten away, and a church spire on the brink of collapse. Even the park in the middle of the village was full of rubble.

"It wasn't like this last week," Kier said with thinly-veiled rage. Power vibrated from him, the ring on his finger spitting sparks of blue light like he couldn't control his magic.

I inched further away from him, not wanting to get struck by any wayward specks of power.

"Has the fog done this?" I asked, watching the village come closer as the carriage rolled, driver-less, down the base of the hill. Behind us, Kier's guards followed on horseback, the manes of the strange, skeletal animals threaded with blue velvet.

"If it has, this is new," Kier replied, practically a growl. His tanned hands curled into fists, knuckles bulging. "I've never seen the Haar do this to a village, only to people."

"Great, so it's mutating. Just what I needed in my new home."

He shot me a sideways look, watchful and surprised if I wasn't reading him wrong. I wondered what part of what I'd said had surprised him.

"Mutating," he echoed. "Magic doesn't mutate."

I made a sound in the back of my throat, not very Orchid-like. But keeping up the frightened bride routine wasn't working; I kept forgetting, letting my true self shine through. I reassessed, amended my plan. Instead of pretending to be someone I wasn't, I'd just be a muted version of myself.

No stabbing, no scaling buildings, no threatening people to their face. But there was no way I could hold back my opinions, even from my despicable husband, so I'd allow myself to speak my mind.

"Maybe it does mutate, and you just haven't been paying attention," I said, looking out the window as the broken, jagged-edged buildings drew near.

When I looked at my husband from the corner of my eye, he looked like he'd chewed a wasp. But he didn't disagree with me.

The carriage rattled past tumbledown shops, their wares visible through broken doors, covered in dust. I saw a box of oranges covered in debris, a dressmaker's mannequin on the ground, a café whose turquoise glass tables were shattered, chairs overturned as if people had fled in a hurry.

All signs of humanity—of ordinary lives. My stomach knotted, my heart speeding. They were people. I should be glad to see evidence of my enemy's suffering, but these weren't soldiers slaughtering my kind on a battlefield. These were *people*, and it sat like a sickness in my stomach.

Something had swept through and devoured these buildings—and when I looked closer, I spotted bleached bones scattered on the ground. The Haar had picked their bones clean, exactly as Xiona had said. Fuck.

"Hey," I said. "I don't suppose you have some of that fog's ruin stuff?"

I expected a belittling speech about not needing it, to stay behind him and cower in his shadow where I'd be safe. But Kier nodded and pulled three vials from the inside pocket of his fancy suit.

"Rook stocked me up," he mumbled, a vague confession to conversation.

"You just keep this stuff on you?" I asked dryly, gratefully accepting the vials and ignoring the spark when his fingers touched mine. If I didn't acknowledge it, it didn't happen. "Were you expecting the Haar to show up to see my announcement as princess?"

"Yes," he grunted. At my raised eyebrow, he growled a sigh and added, "I have a theory that it's controlled by the rebels."

"Ah. The rebels who tried to kill us to stop our wedding. *Those* rebels?"

"Yep. Those bastards."

I searched my dress for somewhere to stash the vials—no fucking pockets, typical—and ended up stashing them down my bosom.

"What?" I demanded when I caught him looking at me with a wry smile on his face. "Where else am I supposed to put them?"

"In a pocket?" he drawled.

"Women aren't given pockets." I gave him the finger,

watched his empty look, and gleefully explained, "The finger means *fuck you.*"

"I don't fuck humans," he laughed scornfully. "I don't trust you; you'll stab me in the back while I sleep."

"In the back, dear husband?" I replied, blinking owlishly. "What about the front?"

I shouldn't have been threatening him. *Definitely* shouldn't have been teasing him with the idea of his own murder. Ugh.

Kier barked a laugh, taking three rings from his pocket —bastard, now he was just boasting about his fucking pockets—and sliding them onto his fingers. Each was capped with a stone in a different colour.

"No sapphires?" I asked, gasping. "Colour me shocked."

The look he threw my way was flat with exasperation. "Mother save me from mouthy wives," he muttered under his breath.

"Wives, plural?" I tilted my head. "How many do you have? Are they stashed in a basement, each behind a locked door? I'll have to liberate them."

"You talk too much," he groaned.

I shrugged. Talking was my current coping mechanism as the condition of the village got worse around us, no longer structures but piles of rubble. Fog streaked thinly through the air, but thicker in the heart of the village. I pressed my hand to my chest, to the reassuring fog's ruin.

"When we go out, stay close to me—" he began

"Ugh, this again. The powerful prince and helpless princess routine." I shot a scathing look at him. I couldn't tell him I could handle myself or he'd reassess me as a threat, but this was starting to piss me off. "I've got fog's ruin, I'm not some wilting flower."

"You're human," he replied, as if that was the same thing.

"Oh, poor me," I muttered. "I'm not a big, strong goblin who can rip heads off with his bare hands." If only he knew all the things I'd done, all the people I'd killed working for Marc the Scythe.

"You can probably *talk* someone to death," he muttered, getting my attention by taking a knife from inside his jacket. It had five gems down the handle, each bezel set and darkest sapphire. My covetous heart fluttered—and skipped when he handed it to me. "But just in case your tongue fails you, have this."

"I thought the Haar could only be stopped by fog's ruin," I mused. "Also, I'm keeping this. Forever. It's mine now." I stroked the sharp edge, my stomach full of butterflies. I couldn't wait to christen this baby.

"It can," he replied grimly, and twisted one of his rings to bring the carriage to a sudden, jolting stop before I could puzzle that answer.

It hit me when I jumped down to the fog-swathed ground, my feet swallowed and hidden by the stuff. I took a vial of fog's ruin from my corset and uncapped it, sprinkling the mist around me and exhaling in relief when it thinned without eating the flesh from my ankles.

The knife wasn't for the fog—it was for the people fighting for their lives within it. In case the goblins decided to murder me while my husband's back was turned.

15

"*R*uthless gods," I swore, swallowing hard as a piercing, desperate scream came from deep within the fog.

Kier grabbed my wrist, uncaring of the knife I held, and dragged me into a sprint in the scream's direction, the guards ploughing into the fog on their horses behind us. I was ready to spray more fog's ruin, but every time Kier's foot struck the hard ground, the fog scattered.

"Okay, what the *hell?*" I asked breathlessly.

He ignored me, focused on the search like a predator scenting prey. He paused only to help a fallen woman out of the fog, the Haar rushing away from where he reached into it.

It was pretty fucking interesting that my husband and his buddies had left out this scrap of information. No wonder Kier had jumped into the fog yesterday. It didn't hurt him. Ran from the sight of him, in fact.

Just this once, staying in his shadow was actually a good idea, so I kept close as he helped another woman to her feet, and then a man, then a group of kids who'd been trying to outrun the Haar's reach. They went pale at the sight of me, as if I was the scary one and not the blue-skinned teenagers.

"It's alright," Kier soothed the kids as their eyes fell on the jewelled dagger in my hand, his voice full of warmth and care. "This is my wife, she's safe."

That's what he thought. I gave him an arch glance. He returned it with a look that dared me to try anything. My mouth twitched. But the smirk slid from my lips when the fog surged higher in the distance, and screams erupted from the thick of it.

"Go," I barked at the kids when they stared, open-mouthed. "*Run*, you idiots."

I wanted to take off with them; it was my instinct to race away from danger, not *towards* it. But Kier didn't hesitate like I did. He plunged deeper down the fog-covered road, and I followed, if only because the Haar fled in his wake, and having a fog-repelling husband was useful.

"You know," I drawled, "a real prince would hide behind his castle walls instead of rushing to save commoners."

Kier made a disgusted sound. "I'm no coward like your human princes."

Clearly. It pissed me the hell off.

"Get behind me," he cut in before I could retort, throwing out an arm.

I held my knife out in front of me, angled to slit someone from balls to throat, but it wasn't a *person* I could cut apart; it was a surge of frothing, furious foam.

The Haar rushed upward into a wave before breaking against a trio of elderly goblin women frantically trying to escape its path.

Kier hissed a word I didn't know, the tone easily recognisable as a swear word, and threw up his hand with a blast of azure light.

"Huh," I said, impressed as one of his rings flared—and darkness shot out of it, combating the Haar wrapping like a snake's tail around the women. "I want one of those things," I decided.

Magic freaked me out, but I was in a new world now, and I was playing by its rules. If I didn't adapt, I'd get eaten by the Haar.

Kier snorted, but he reached into his jacket and passed me a tiny signet ring with a sapphire in a carved dragon's eye.

"Thanks," I said awkwardly, not sure why he kept giving me things. I slid the ring onto my finger—of course the only finger it fit was where a wedding ring would traditionally sit —and rolled my eyes at the women who'd frozen in shock.

"Come on," I huffed, stalking over to them, scattering fog with fog's ruin. "Don't stay here, you'll get eaten."

A tan-skinned woman went pale at the sight of me. Exasperated, I said, "Zabaletta, new princess of your kingdom. Here to help."

Oh, how the mighty had fallen. Two days ago I'd been a part-time assassin, full-time figurehead-in-training. Now, I was *helping* people. Ugh, my reputation would never recover. In some parts of Seagrave they called me the Dagger of Night; if word reached home of me becoming a princess and good Samaritan, no one would ever take me seriously again.

But there was always the book deal in my future. A Month With A Murderer—that's what I'd call it. It might have been hypocritical, given I was a killer too, but it was a catchy title, and you couldn't deny that.

"Head up that way," I told the gawking women, pointing to where we'd come from. "The fog's thinner there. Or you can stay here and get eaten," I added with a huff. "Totally up to you."

"Thank you," a blue-toned, grey-haired woman said emphatically, clasping my hand and pumping it with her own. Ugh. People were *touching* me now? Why were people *touching* me? My face usually warned people against that sort of thing. Don't tell me my shiny new title had rendered my glare of warning useless. "Thank you, princess."

"No problem," I replied cavalierly, extricating my hand and honestly grateful when a guard slid off her horse to come to my side, thin red braids slapping her back when she landed.

A bit late if you asked me—I could have been stabbed by now—but I appreciated the back-up. Give me an armed madman to kill or a mansion to break into, and I'd be in my element. But people? *Thanking* me? Looking at me with a mix of awe and gratitude?

"Come on, girls," the old woman said to her two friends, and it hit me, just then, how weird it was that we had a common language. We all spoke the same words, no difference in language except for that one curse Kier had spat. Everything else had been the same language we spoke in Lucre.

"Talon," the guard said, striding alongside me deeper into the fog. I'd lost my damn mind for going deeper into the Haar, but I couldn't get the strange oily sensation of the woman's thanks out of my head. People—they were just people.

"Where?" I asked, warily scanning the fog twisting around my knees. Fuck, it was rising higher. Where the hell had Kier vanished to?

"It's my name," she explained, her voice clipped and no-nonsense.

"Oh, right." I gave her a nod of greeting, striding through

the fog and wondering if it would eat through my shoes if I stayed here long enough. "Zabaletta; nice to meet you."

I paused, my ears straining towards a sound to my right. "Do you hear something?" I asked Talon, my head cocked to the side.

"Whimpering," she replied a moment later, her dark face taut with sternness.

"Ruthless gods," I sighed, and ploughed deeper into the Haar, my dagger out in front of me for all the good it would do and the vial of fog's ruin in my other hand. I scattered drops of the syrupy mixture as we walked, the Haar thinning around us so I could see my knees even if my feet were blanketed. "I don't suppose you saw where my husband went?"

"No," Talon confirmed, striding beside me. Her long legs should have carried her far ahead, but she kept pace, looking like she'd punch the Haar in its face if it had one. I didn't want to get on her bad side. If she hunted me down for killing her prince ... actually, I didn't want to finish that thought.

"Hello?" I called, squinting through the opaque fog. I yelped when lightning-like magic flashed through the fluffy forms curling along the ground. "If you can hear me, shout 'help.'"

"What?" I asked at Talon's sideways look. "If you have a more apt word, I'm all ears."

A thready voice rose in the distance, barely more than a whimper, but I adjusted my course, skirting the corner of a ruined building. A glance into its smoky rooms revealed boxes and jars full of plants, herbs, and muslin. A healer's shop.

Ah, shit, not the fucking healers. If anything was sacred among humans, it was gods and healers. Anger throbbed through my chest at the sight of it, and I stalked ahead faster, cutting at the Haar with my dagger.

"Careful," Talon warned, edging closer to me. It made my hackles rise, and I gave her a warning glance to keep her out of my personal space. She ignored it, inflated on her duty and purpose. She was going to be a serious pain in my backside.

I flung fog's ruin in front of me and strode through the scattering Haar, reaching for another vial. The whimpering was louder around a corner, so I sped up—and hissed when I hit the edge of a curb, going flying.

Like a valiant knight, Talon caught me, pulling me against her body. If she'd been human, I'd have been halfway in love with her. She was a hundred percent my type—broody, secretive, dangerous, alphahole-ish. Shame about the goblin part.

"If you wanted to feel my body, all you had to do was ask," I purred, enjoying the flash of shock on her face. So she wasn't opposed to flirty women, but baulked at how to respond. Good to know. When I killed Kier, I could flirt my way to safety.

I moved away from Talon and stalked down a crumbled alleyway—but carefully, testing the ground for hazards.

"Hello?" I called down the path.

A sob answered me, and then a small blur shot down the alley and collided with my legs. It took me a moment to realise it was a *kid*, and then I swore viciously. Goblin or not, there wasn't a thing in any world that could stop me bending to pick up that kid and propping them on my hip. He was no older than five, and must have been completely submerged in the carnivorous fog when I found him.

"Are you okay?" I asked, scanning the boy from indigo head to toe. He was missing a shoe, but everything else looked intact, and he seemed healthy enough. There was no way to tell if he was pale given his blue skin, but he was certainly terrified. He threw both arms around my neck and clung hard.

"I don't like the fog," he said in a small voice.

"Me either," I agreed, transferring my knife into my other hand so I could keep him secure on my hip. I tore the stopper out of the vial with my teeth, spitting it onto the ground and spraying the street beyond the alley with fog's ruin.

"That's littering," he complained.

"Hey, I just saved you." I shot him an amused smirk. "Now you're lecturing me?"

"But it *is* littering. My mum says that's bad."

"She's not wrong, kid." I exchanged a glance with Talon, who hung back watching the street. "Find us a way out of this thing," I told her. Ordered her, I realised when she nodded briskly and guided us back up the street. She respected my authority as princess. That was strange. Kinda cool, but strange.

"You feel weird," the kid commented, and sniffed my neck. "And you smell funny."

"Thanks," I drawled. "You're just full of compliments today, huh? Aren't princesses supposed to be told they're pretty?"

"You are pretty," he replied, squinting at me through the thin mist at shoulder level. Wait, was it getting higher? "But you smell funny."

Talon snorted, like she couldn't hold in the sound. "You smell human," she explained, holding a hand out to guide us down a different street, the buildings reduced to nothing here. There weren't even hints of what these had been, just smears on the ground to mark where buildings had once stood and ash blowing in the soft wind. The Haar's fog drifted higher, and I swallowed.

I flicked my wrist to throw more fog's ruin, and realised the vial was empty. The kid tutted as I threw the empty glass aside and prised the last one from my corset.

"Get behind me," Talon growled, so suddenly primal that I flinched, gasping roughly.

With the vial and my dagger balanced awkwardly in one hand, I couldn't defend myself, and it took my panicked instincts too fucking long to realise it wasn't Talon that was the threat—but the silver-shot fog growing denser, tighter around us.

"What's that sound?" I breathed, a low humming grating the edges of my nerves.

"I don't know," Talon said on a snarl. "I've never heard it before."

The kid whimpered, pressing his face to my neck.

"Hey," I breathed, softening my voice. "What's your name, kid?"

"Ari," he whispered, like he was scared the Haar would hear him.

"You're gonna be fine, Ari. I won't let the fog get you." It didn't matter that he was a goblin, and I was human. We weren't enemies; he was a baby for fuck's sake. I didn't like the questions that raised, or the way my stomach twisted. I'd deal with that later, if I made it out of this nightmare.

Sweat dripped down the back of my dress at the electric press of the fog. It rushed up against me like ocean waves on a shore, or a very persistent cat. I dumped the whole vial of fog's ruin, taking a step—and freezing when the Haar didn't scatter like it had before.

"*Run*, your highness," Talon growled, drawing a necklace from beneath her uniform, a fat tanzanite hanging in a frame of silver. Magic burst to life in its heart, and she sliced her hand at the fog—to no effect whatsoever.

I glanced at the ring on my own hand as I let the empty vial shatter at my feet. I heard it, but couldn't see a thing through the thick white fog, lightning sparking and flashing around us so suddenly that I jumped back, my heart hammering.

"How do you work those things?" I demanded, clutching Ari tighter to my chest as I backed up a step. The Haar pressed even closer at my retreat. It had a solid weight despite being fucking *fog*, like it had a body. I shuddered.

Talon glanced askance at me, and I jerked my chin at her necklace as she lifted it, aiming another burst of blue magic into the fog. It swallowed the blast whole, not even flinching. Certainly not scattering like it had at the fog's ruin earlier. Even if the syrupy stuff had *zero* effect now.

The thing I liked about Talon despite knowing her less than an hour was she didn't question me. She didn't ask *why* I wanted to know how the magic worked; she just said, clear and brisk, "I picture the shape I want it to take and imagine the effect of the power as if it's a foregone conclusion."

She glanced my way and saw me lift my hand, the signet ring warm on my finger.

"It won't work," Talon said hesitantly. "Humans have no magic. Even with marriage, you wouldn't be able to call on it. Only if you were—"

She stuttered into silence as bright, pure blue unfurled from the ring on my finger.

"Oooh," Ari breathed, lifting his head off my shoulder at the light show erupting from my ring.

I was well used to acting like things were foregone conclusions; leaping from roof to roof only worked if you acted like catching the opposite building would be no problem. Sneaking through windows only worked if you acted sure and confident, regardless of guard dogs, security shields, and bodyguards. Magic was no different, and it twisted my stomach up at how *readily* it came from the ring. Like it had been waiting for me to use it.

Daggers of richest blue flashed through the air and sank into the magic, and for five seconds I felt incredibly pleased with myself. Magic might have been terrifying, but much like guns, it felt good to be on the other end of it. I felt powerful. At least until the fog swallowed my magic like it was nothing.

"Hey!" I complained—and I swore the Haar throbbed around us. It rushed closer to me, throwing Talon aside so suddenly that the guard was knocked off her feet. Her red braids were the last thing I saw before her uniformed body was swallowed by flashing fog.

"Give me my guard back," I growled.

Ari wasn't *ooh*ing at my magic anymore; he had his face buried in my neck and he shook as he clung to me. Where the hell were his parents? Had they been picked clean by the Haar? Fuck, if he was an orphan, things were about to become very inconvenient for me; I was already attached to him.

"Back off," I growled at the fog, taking a backward step and nearly falling as the Haar pressed against my thighs, more like a circling panther than a cat now.

I brought that visual to life and sent an azure panther exploding from the ring on my finger, sinking teeth and claws into the fog. It was a toddler-sized panther, but it still counted. It was cool as fuck.

A shudder skated down my spine at the low, rumbling laugh that echoed all around me. I went cold all over. Was ... was the Haar *laughing* at me?

Breathing was suddenly a difficult task. I backed up, holding Ari close, almost strangled by the death grip his indigo arms had around my neck. The press of the fog was stifling, suffocating. I swallowed roughly as the fog rushed higher, lapping at my shoulders, almost covering Ari.

I stumbled back a step, but the smoke was everywhere, obsessive and endless. I was going to die here, eaten to death by *fog* of all things, in the land of my enemy. And I hadn't even killed Kier Kollastus yet.

I hissed, furious and terrified, shaking all over as a tendril of fog brushed my chin, and ran creepy fingers along my bottom lip. I braced for it to shove down my throat, choke me to death, and—

The Haar shrieked and scattered, the low purr of its laughter cutting out as it fled.

The relief I felt was sickening.

Bile rushed into my throat at the taste of gratitude on my tongue, and I swallowed hard as Kier strode through the fog, unflinching as he aimed for me.

"Don't," I sighed at the rage on his face, exhausted and shaky.

"What the hell were—"

He drew up short at the sight of Ari lifting his head off my shoulder, his obscenely blue face peering at my husband. Ari's eyes went comically wide and he shot me a panicked look.

"It's the prince. We should bow," he whispered.

"*You* can bow," I replied with as much humour as I could dredge up. "I'm not gonna bother."

The kid looked at me like I'd gone mad, or had a death wish, or both.

"You're holding a goblin child," Kier commented, recovering from his shock as he closed the last bit of distance between us, his eyes taking an intense sweep down my body.

"Yeah, this is Ari. Ari, say hi."

Ari squeaked out, "He's the prince!"

"Wait until you find out who I am," I replied with a breathy laugh, ignoring the way Kier watched me, noting every sign of my fright.

"You went into the Haar to rescue a goblin child," Kier said, prowling even closer.

I straightened. He'd never been this close to me before, not even for that sham of a kiss. As if in memory, my lips prickled, and I bit my bottom lip before I caught myself and released it.

"Yeah," I said, hairs rising on the back of my neck when Kier's blue eyes darkened to almost black. He held me captive with those eyes, and I couldn't move a step. "And?"

"*Ariven!*" a woman screamed, panic a bright star in her voice.

Both Kier and I jumped, and I shook free of whatever the hell *that* had been.

"Sounds like your mum's looking for you, kid," I said with relief. I didn't have the time to be adopting an orphan; thank *fuck* he had a parent. "Let's get you home, yeah?"

I ignored the dark, heady way Kier watched me cross the street, the fog thinning as he followed, scattering the Haar in his wake. In that moment, I didn't care why it responded like that, only that I wasn't going to get eaten alive by the damn thing.

"Mum!" Ari yelled when we spotted the silver-haired blue woman, her long dress covered in dust and dark with blood in patches. He wriggled in my arms, and I set him free when I was sure he wouldn't be swallowed by the Haar.

"Mother's mercy," Ari's mum choked out, rushing to meet him halfway and gathering him into her arms.

I ignored the way my heart panged, my parents little more than a memory.

"Thank you," the woman breathed, glancing up at me—and staring with the same comically wide eyes as her son when she spotted Kier.

She bowed instantly, her head low and respectful. "Thank you, your highness—es," she amended, correctly guessing my identity.

"No problem," I replied before my husband could take credit. "He's a good kid."

I shuddered at a touch to my hair. Kier curled a messy strand around his finger, lazily sliding it all the way to the ends of my hair. My stomach tightened, my breath quickening.

"Thank you," the woman breathed, still bowing even as she grabbed Ari close and backed away. "Thank you."

"I'm glad the smoke didn't eat us," Ari said innocently, startling a tense laugh from my swiftly-closing throat.

"Me too, kid."

"And don't litter!" he called as his mum ushered him up the road towards where the fog was thinner.

"No promises."

I didn't turn away from their retreating backs for a long time. I liked to think I was a brave person, but I was *petrified* of what I'd face when I looked at my hateful husband. My sister's killer.

I was more scared of why my heart beat fast, and why my scalp tingled at that light touch to my hair.

I hated him with every fibre of my being. I turned slowly, warily.

"I'm disgustingly attracted to you right now," he hissed, eyes black and nostrils flaring.

Oh god, if goblins had some advanced scent nonsense... I was ashamed of myself, ashamed of my body's response.

"Likewise," I bit out, my teeth bared. "I hate you so much."

His mouth flicked up, his sharp-planed face taut with desire and revulsion. "The feeling, Zabaletta, is mutual."

He loomed over me, and I didn't know how the hell I'd talk myself out of this—I was *his wife*, after all.

Feet scuffed the ground, startling us apart. Talon dragged herself into the road, clutching the twisted remnants of a streetlight, and I'd never been more glad to see her.

I stumbled away from Kier, my heart slamming against my ribs and my stomach rushing with sickness.

"How in the Mother's realm did you do that?" Talon demanded, stalking up to me with a wild look on her face.

"I didn't do anything. It was all him." I hooked a thumb in Kier's direction.

"No. Your power, the *magic*—I saw the panther." Talon looked undone, her eyes startled and her black-scale uniform chewed up in places by the fog.

Kier spun to face me again, even as he helped support Talon across the street.

"Ah," I breathed, shifting my weight. "Yeah. Turns out I can use magic, too."

"That's impossible," Kier growled, all evidence that he'd wanted me wiped away. Thank fuck for that.

Talon shook her head, disagreeing. "Not if you're bond-mates."

16

"*S*tart talking," I ordered Talon, crossing my arms over my chest as Kier silently stalked off. To brood, probably. "What the *hell* is a bond-mate?"

"We should go back to the carriage," Talon said, giving me a stoic look and herding me up the street.

I followed, if only for answers and because I didn't want to stay in this wrecked village for much longer.

"*Talk*, lady. I'm your princess; isn't there some law against not answering my questions?"

Her mouth pressed thin, but she relented. "A bond-mate is exactly what it sounds like. Two or more people whose souls are twined together."

Perfect. I sucked on a tooth, stalking up the sloped road. "So how do I undo it?"

"*Undo* it?" Talon burst out, incredulous as she gaped at me. Her broad shoulders bristled, brown skin showing through the slashes and holes in her dragon-scale uniform. "A mating bond is a gift from the Mother. Someone who's the perfect fit for you in every way—physically, mentally, emotionally, and on a *soul* level. Denying your mate is like carving out your lungs. He's an essential part of you."

I suppressed a snort, but barely. There had to be a way to undo it if we really *had* been bound together; this sounded like more magic bullshit, and all magic could be reversed. Right?

We reached the top of the hill, the Haar thinned so much that we could see the ruin of the village. Streets were lucky if they had three buildings left standing; most had crumbled entirely.

"What will happen to the people who live here?" I asked, remembering Ari and his mother. I held a knife to the throat of my conscience to keep it quiet, but it didn't seem to be working.

"They'll move further inland to places the Haar hasn't reached yet."

She gestured me towards the carriage; I dragged my feet just in case my husband waited inside. I didn't like the idea of being in such close confines with him with all this bond-mate nonsense hanging over me.

It was bad enough being married to my sister's killer. At least I could endure that knowing he'd be dead at the end of the month. But having his soul twisted into mine, poisoning me with his hateful goblin magic? My skin crawled.

"But what will happen to this village?" I pressed Talon, pausing outside the carriage and looking at the mess that had been people's homes this morning. "Will it be rebuilt?"

"The Haar will return; it always does. There are other villages, and cities far bigger than Lazankh that have been abandoned. They belong to the Haar now; even fog's ruin or his highness's presence can't keep it away forever. Every week, it takes more land from us."

She said every chilling fact with a sort of detachment.

She was the stoic knight through and through—except for the flash of bright red in her braids, which hinted at a personality her uniform couldn't hide. Were goblins really so used to this fog devouring their homes and people that they could sound so unruffled about it? People had *died* here. They'd been eaten by the fog, with only skeletons left behind. And now the lucky survivors were forced to move to a different village, and live fuck knows where. Would people take them in? Or would they live on the streets?

I shouldn't give a shit, but injustice made my temper fiery hot.

I grabbed the carriage door and wrenched it open, levelling a glare on my brooding husband as his dark head snapped up. He met my eyes with a scowl simmering with rage. Good, that made two of us.

"Nice meeting you, Talon," I said with a sharp nod, and hauled myself up into the carriage, slamming the door shut. "Hello, husband," I greeted, halfway between a purr and snarl.

His gaze sharpened, eyes flashing with dark interest as I threw myself onto the blue bench opposite him.

"You're a bullshit prince," I told him, panic at the mate thing snarled up with anger on behalf of his people. "These people are supposed to just leave their village and travel to another place, with no guarantee of shelter, income, or support?"

Surprise widened his blue-black eyes, and he leaned back in his seat, resting his foot on his opposite knee. "You're angry because the Haar destroyed the village?"

"I'm angry because you're *letting* it," I hissed back, watching the ring on my finger spit blue sparks. "Talon told me you allow the fog to claim the places it eats—you just move out whatever people manage to survive and leave the lands to the Haar. *What the fuck,* Kier?"

He tilted his head slowly, black hair falling across his shoulder. "That's the first time you've said my name."

"Useless," I hissed, inhaling sharply through gritted teeth when the carriage set off without warning, rattling over the pockmarked road.

"Would I be here if I was useless?" he asked, dark eyes pinned on me as he twisted a ring around his finger. "Would I have scoured the fog to be sure there were no more survivors, and ordered my guard to escort them to the next safest village?"

"How big of you," I replied with acidic sweetness. "How *generous*—to tell your servants to help them instead of doing it yourself. Afraid to get your hands dirty with the masses, your highness?"

Kier flashed his teeth at me. "I do what I can. There's no way to stop the Haar, only to hold it back long enough to get people out. We arrived here too late to save the village, but even if we hadn't, it would sweep back in. Like the ocean eating at cliffs day by day—it never relents."

"So how long until it eats your pretty castle?" I asked, crossing my arms over my chest, dagger still clenched in my fist.

He growled—fiercely enough that I tensed, watching him closely. One false move, and he'd find himself bleeding from a stab wound, goblin moon or no goblin moon.

"You think I don't know that?" he demanded, his tanned face taut with rage. "I'm doing everything I can to hold back the tide, but nothing we've tried is enough."

"Then try something else."

"If you have any suggestions, I'm all ears," he bit out.

I eyed his slightly pointed ears, the one indicator that he

was a goblin in human form. "Evacuate people now, before the Haar's path reaches them. Build temporary housing until you can find a way to get rid of this fucking thing. And use all your power as a goblin royal—all the power Rook bragged you have—to kill the damn Haar. Easy peasy."

Kier rolled his eyes up to the roof of the carriage and laughed, a low rumble. I calmed myself with the picture of my jewelled blade sinking into his throat, blood spurting everywhere, drenching the floor of the carriage.

"In every bit of my spare time, I research ways to end the Haar," he said finally, his voice subdued but still threaded with fury. "I search our histories for *any* record of this happening before. I've tried every gemstone, every bit of power I have in my veins, and *nothing* has worked. I'm doing everything I can."

He expelled a breath, clenching his hands into fists. "But you're right about everything else. We'll set up a village for refugees, and I'll make sure evacuations begin the second we get home."

My rage skipped a step.

Huh? *What?*

He'd heard me, listened, and would do what I suggested?

"So you care about your people dying, but you'll walk onto a battlefield and slaughter hundreds?" I asked, my heart beating harder, a thump against my ribs that growled *he killed Natasya* with every slam.

"I've never been on a battlefield," Kier replied with a furrow between dark eyes. "Why would you think I had?"

I blinked fast, shaking my head. "Bullshit."

Why else would he shred my sister's body to blood and bones? Why, if not because they met in combat? The demand hovered on the tip of my tongue—*tell me why you killed my sister. Why did you kill Natasya Stellara?*

He was lying—why else would he do what he'd done? There were witnesses who saw him—exactly him—throw Natasya's body on the edge of Seagrave.

"I've trained for it," he went on, messing with his rings. "But I've never been called to the front. Not yet, anyway," he added with a grimace, dragging a hand through his hair. "With the way this war's going, I'll be called up within months."

He seemed to realise he was talking to a human, to the enemy, and fell silent.

"But there are stories of you fighting," I murmured, a spike of pain going through my heart. If I'd married him for nothing, if he *wasn't* Natasya's murderer...

Kier scoffed, shaking his head. "Stories to spook the humans. They're more afraid of the lords, princes, and the king."

"Princes, plural?" I asked, ignoring the venomous way he said humans. "Your brothers?"

He nodded, a muscle fluttering in his jaw. I sensed they didn't get along too well. "Two of them. Bastards."

I snorted, beginning to calm from my earlier rage, even if I felt sick at the idea of him never fighting on a battlefield. He could be lying. I wanted to believe he was lying.

"About this mate shit," I said, forcing myself to say it aloud. "It's not real, right? There's no way our souls are magically perfect for each other. You hate me, I hate you."

His mouth flicked into a smirk. "If we *are* mates, it'll be disastrous. It has to be a fluke. Maybe your power came from the Haar."

A shiver of revulsion went down my spine. "It laughed at me."

Kier narrowed his eyes, meeting my stare. "The Haar

can't laugh. It doesn't have a voice—it's fog and power, nothing more."

"I'm telling you," I insisted, my temper spiking again as I leaned forward, glaring at him. "It fucking *laughed* at me, and then it ate my jaguar."

Kier sighed, gaze drifting to the sapphire ring on my finger, noticing which finger I'd placed it on. "Maybe Talon laughed."

I gave him a flat stare. "Have you met the woman? I don't think she's ever *heard* of laughing. She probably thinks smiling is a myth, and laughter is something the kids made up to fuck with her."

"The Haar doesn't laugh," he insisted, ignoring my argument.

"But—" I began, waving my dagger.

"The Haar *doesn't* laugh," he repeated, firm enough to kill the conversation.

I narrowed my eyes and fell silent, planning his death. By the wary look he threw my way, he might have realised it.

I knew what I'd heard, and now I was sure Kier Kollastus was a liar as well as a murderer. There was something more to the Haar, and while I waited for the goblin moon, I might as well figure out what my dear husband was hiding.

17

*T*rue to her word, Calanthe came for me the next morning with a promise of a tour of the castle and the City of Sapphires. My mood lifted as I threw the silken bed covers back and climbed out, my new nightdress tumbling down my thighs in a luxurious fabric.

I'd come home yesterday to find the wardrobe full of elegant dresses in a dozen jewel tones and rich fabrics, and the drawers teeming with shirts, soft leggings, tights, frilly socks, and scarves that, while pretty, would do nothing to keep out the biting cold. Still, Calanthe had outdone herself, and I was grateful for the new clothes even if I really didn't want to know who'd paid for them. The idea of wearing gifts from Kier Kollastus, prince of goblins and killer of my sister...

You almost kissed him yesterday, a cruel voice said with all the precision and violence of a knife wound, *and you're worried about taking* gifts *from him?*

I shut out the words, throwing open the wardrobe doors as Calanthe laid a breakfast tray on my table and said, "You should hear the buzz around the castle. Everyone's talking about the new village prince Kier is building."

"*Having* built," I corrected, slipping behind a beautiful wooden screen and pushing the straps of my slip off my shoulders, letting the silk pool on the floor as I reached for underwear and contemplated the wardrobe.

"What's the difference?" Calanthe asked.

"He's not doing the work himself."

There were two pairs of trousers—just two. Both were starched and pressed within an inch of their lives, but I wanted more freedom of movement for exploring the city. Besides, dresses were *heavy*. I'd already dragged one around for hours yesterday; I refused to do the same today, so I grabbed a pair of stiff navy blue trousers and a soft cotton shirt in warm cream.

"Ruthless gods," I laughed, pulling the shirt over my bust with immense effort. "These clothes are a bit tight."

"They should be perfectly fitted to your form," Calanthe replied with a furrow between her hazel eyes. She bustled over as I stepped out from behind the screen, the cotton hugging my boobs so tightly they were shoved up by my throat.

Calanthe blinked, her mouth twitching. "You're sure to garner attention, at least."

I faked a scandalised gasp. "Calanthe! I'm a married woman."

Her smirk deepened, lighting up her freckled face. Gods, she was pretty. And the woman she loved had rejected her? Madwoman. "I meant your *husband's* attention," she said wryly.

I turned away, tugging at my shirt before I gave up and unfastened the top button, giving my boobs some breathing room.

"You two have ... consummated your marriage?" Calanthe asked hesitantly, chewing on her full bottom lip. "Right?"

"Of course," I replied, not too fast, not too defensively. Thank gods for my street urchin upbringing and Celandrine's training. If nothing else, I was a talented wielder of total bullshit. "But only once."

"Ah," she replied sadly, leaning her curvy hip against the table as she watched me. "The prince always struck me as slow to trust, especially after that business with his brothers. Just give him time. Or make the first move—but carefully."

"You talk about him like he's a spooked dog," I said dryly, and left enough time to not seem too greedy for information before asking, "He has brothers?"

I knew that—he'd told me himself—but my gossip senses were alive with curiosity.

"Two," Calanthe replied, moving to the curtains to straighten them—no knives were hidden there today, I'd found more creative and sustainable hiding places—before attacking the messy covers. "They're not on good terms. Their sister died five years ago; she was only young, poor thing. Eight, I think. It fractured Prince Kier's relationship with the rest of his family."

She shot me a look, tugging the sheet into place. "But I didn't tell you this."

I gave her a grin. "Tell me what? All I hear is birdsong."

Calanthe snorted, finishing her abuse of the covers before changing the pillow cases with an efficiency I envied.

"Danette was always a sickly child. Bright and as sharp as a pin from what I've heard, but weak. Prince Kier brought her here so she'd have the forest and mountains nearby, and so the healing stone in the castle's highest tower might grant her a longer life."

I crossed my arms over my chest, shoving down the sympathy and understanding that rose as Calanthe spoke. My own grief stabbed through my chest and into my heart, but at least I'd had twenty-two years with Natasya. Kier had only had eight years with Danette.

"I didn't know there was a healing stone in the castle," I said, smothering my pain with a warm roll of sugar-spiced bread. "I don't remember seeing anything in the tower." Unless it was tiny and I'd never spot it from the carriage.

Calanthe shook her head sadly, but something fiercer chased across her freckled face. "Danette's condition improved while she was here, under his highness's care and near the healing stone. But an elite team of humans broke through the border and crossed the mountains."

I straightened, choking down the bite of bread in my mouth. I knew where this was going.

"They thought it was a battle stone, and stealing it would weaken our soldiers." Calanthe spat a bitter laugh, shaking her curly head. "Idiots. Fucking fools."

It was the first time she'd sworn in my presence, and I blinked. I grabbed a glass of water and took a sip to settle my stomach. "The humans stole the stone, and she died, didn't she?"

"She did," Calanthe confirmed with a heavy sigh. "And Prince Kier has never been the same again. His family … they blame him for her death. Even though no one could have seen those sly humans coming."

"So that's why he hates humans," I mused, hating that I understood, that it was a mirror image of my own grief.

"Humans in general, but not you," Calanthe countered, her voice softening with an attempt at comfort.

I waved a hand; I didn't want pretty lies. But I was glad to know a kernel of truth. "I understand why he would. I would, too."

I do, too.

"Ready to go explore?" I asked, clumsily changing the subject. I didn't like the feelings churning inside me, didn't want to examine them at all.

Calanthe's expression brightened, her eyes glittering. "I have *so* much to show you. But um, what are you going to do about ... them?"

She gestured at my tight shirt, where my cleavage was basically spilling out. I shrugged, propping my hands on my hips and striking a pose. "Nothing. Might as well give my people something to brighten their day."

Calanthe grinned, her eyes practically disappearing as her cheeks rounded.

I shoved away the feeling of creeping unease, hunted down suitable footwear for a day of adventuring, and left all thoughts of sympathy and understanding in the bedroom, firmly closing the door behind myself.

18

*T*here were gemstones everywhere around the castle. Calanthe pointed out each one, and explained their purpose while I stared in awe or narrowed my eyes in distrust.

One was for sweeping dust from the floor, another for making the stained-glass windows gleam brightly in their palette of blues, and one for heating the air to the perfect temperature. Another played soft harp music when activated, the sapphire beside it fortifying the castle walls with magic so they could never be broken, and the giant, carriage-sized tanzanite above the grand castle steps covered the whole city of Lazankh in a shimmery blue shield that, in theory, repelled attack.

It clearly did nothing against thieves and trickery, or the healing stone wouldn't have been stolen years ago. Still, it was hard not to be impressed with all the protections on the castle. Apparently there were even more stones of power around the private royal rooms, keeping Kier safe during the goblin moon.

"So no one can hurt him during the moon?" I asked as carefully as possible.

Calanthe patted my arm with a warm brown hand; she'd long since lost her fight against her tactile nature even if I *was* a princess and way above her maid status. She could be a good friend, I realised with a pang of regret. She'd hate me when she knew I'd used her kindness.

"No one will get past the shields; that's what they're for. The only person who could hurt Prince Kier during that time is himself, but you'll be there to keep him safe."

I exhaled a rough breath, pretending relief, and watched the gold-liveried staff pass us with sharp, observant eyes. A plan formed in my mind as Calanthe went on to explain the history of the various doors around the castle. If I could get my hands on one of those golden uniforms, I could dump it in Kier's room once I'd killed him. Anyone would see it and think someone had snuck into the castle in disguise. Better yet, if I could make it look like I'd been kidnapped, I'd be out of the picture.

Humans had broken in once; who was to say rebels couldn't get in again?

"Here we are, then," Calanthe said proudly, her warm face split with a beaming grin as she bounced on her heels in front of a grubby looking door.

"Wow, this is my favourite landmark yet," I drawled, smirking at her bright laugh. "I've always wanted to go on a sightseeing tour of a cellar; how did you know?"

She laid a hand over her heart, playing along. "I'd be an awful lady's maid if I didn't know your innermost desires."

Good thing she didn't know my actual desires. "We don't pay you nearly enough, Calanthe."

"I know," she laughed, gesturing for me to open the door.

My gaze flat, I grabbed the cold iron handle and tugged

it open—gasping in genuine surprise when a vibrant market spread out on the other side. Scents of sweet honey and earthy spices met my nose, followed by slow-roasting meat, perfumed flowers, and burning wood.

Calanthe laughed at the expression on my face, looking mightily pleased with herself. Fair enough; she ought to be.

"Okay, I'm impressed," I admitted, staring at the people moving among the brightly painted stalls, their blue canvas tarpaulins flapping in the wind through the mountains. Each of them was ladened with food, fabric, pottery, art, and leather goods.

Calanthe curtsied with a grin at the compliment. "Shall we go?"

"Hell, yes."

I stepped through the cellar doorway into the market with a grin on my face. Markets were full of people—full of *information*. If I was going to find the truth about the Haar and the goblin moon anywhere, it would be here.

19

"*M*y feet hurt," I complained, biting into a lump of deep-fried dough shaped into a dragon's head and dipped in sugar. I missed my rubber climbing shoes, abandoned in the alleyway near the dress-maker's shop in Merikand. Gods, I even missed the low-heeled boots Celandrine had us wearing to train in. The flat boots I wore now had nothing in the way of comfort or support.

"You need some of these," Calanthe replied, clicking the heels of her shoes together. "I can walk for miles in these things."

I cast a dubious look at the beige monstrosities on her feet. "But they're *ugly*."

She laughed, leading me past a row of booths where vendors called out 'better-than-ever' offers that miracu-lously became *even* better when they recognised me.

"A whole bolt of velvet just for you, princess," a deep-voiced woman shouted. "I'll do it for twelve silver fangs."

I pretended not to hear. I had more than enough velvet in the wardrobe at the castle. What I needed was leather, but it would be hard to explain why I needed that to Calanthe. She might have been my maid, might have answered to me, but I had no doubt that her eyes watched me on behalf of the royals, Kier especially.

I ate the last of my deep-fried dragon, sucking the sugar off my fingers, and winked at a scrawny man in his early twenties I caught staring. Why goblins were so obsessed with dragons, I didn't know. I saw images of them everywhere.

A loud cheer caught my attention, and I steered Calanthe in that direction, a surprised smile crossing my face when I saw a trio of street performers decked out in bright, garish costumes. A crowd of shoppers circled the performers, kids bouncing excitedly as the show began.

From the corner of my eye, I watched a black-clad guard edge closer—three of them had been shadowing us from the moment we entered the market. Our tour of the city had been vetoed, with Dove—and presumably the head of security—compromising on a market visit with armed guards. If I wanted to explore the city and find silversweet to make my own supply of fog's ruin, I'd have to sneak out and make my own exploration.

"I didn't know you guys had performers," I said, and then realised how fucking ignorant that sounded. I aimed a wince at Calanthe but she only smiled and nodded, not judging me. I still had a backward vision of goblins, but the more time I spent in their kingdom, the more I was realising they weren't too different from humans. Not when they weren't bright blue anyway.

Although Ali and his mum were challenging those beliefs, too.

"There's a troupe who travel through all the major cities," Calanthe told me with genuine enthusiasm. I wondered if she might dream of joining them, her gleaming eyes pinned on the three performers as they rattled bells to hush the crowd.

One man was dressed in pure white, but the others were dressed in garish colours, royal blue and gaudy gold, aqua and orange. Both wore cheap tin crowns, one vaguely more impressive than the other.

"Oh!" Calanthe breathed, her freckled face lighting up. "It's the story of the Haar."

Convenient.

I crossed my arms over my chest—making sure I wasn't accidentally flashing the crowd when a button popped open —and tried not to grin. I'd been trying to find a way to press for information about the fog, and here a performance had landed in my lap.

"How truthful is it?" I asked, watching our guard slide into the path of a silver-haired goblin man, rerouting him. Did he want to garner my favour, or to seduce me away from Kier? I gave him a cursory look; not my type. Too clean cut.

"The beginning's exactly as it happened, but the ending is imagined." Calanthe fell silent with a quick inhale as the crowned players stretched out a giant piece of fabric painted with a pastoral scene.

I leaned forward for a closer look and I swore the grasses on the hills moved in an invisible wind. It did! There were tiny, opaque white gemstones sewn into the fabric, magic making the scene come to life.

I glanced at the ring on my finger, as if it would flash in response to the performer's magic. It stayed dead, gleaming dark blue.

"Watch this," Calanthe urged, so I returned my attention to the troupe as the white-clad figure—the Haar, presum- ably—pirouetted in front of the crowd, mist trailing in his wake. I pinpointed a jade gem in his earring, the smoke unfurling from it to create the effect of the Haar.

The crowd shifted uneasily around me. How many of them had lost friends and family from neighbouring villages? I cast a glance around, reading the energy and atmosphere of the people. My people. Ugh, that wasn't a pleasant thought.

"The Haar crept in overnight," the player with the bigger crown said in an amplified voice. "Like a stalker in the dark, it hunts our villages and people. But if it thinks goblins are easy prey, it's badly mistaken."

A few of the people around us nodded, muttering. The kids didn't look as enthusiastic anymore, but when the Haar backflipped—for no apparent reason—past the painted village, scattering mist everywhere, the player with the smaller crown booed and the kids joined in. Clever, to turn their biggest enemy into a pantomime villain.

I tilted my head, watching the performance play out. So the Haar had appeared without warning.

"As if the death of our beloved princess hadn't hurt us enough," the narrator—the King, I realised—continued with pomp and drama, "the Haar swallowed our villages the same week. Stole our people."

"This is cheery," I said under my breath.

Calanthe shot me an amused look. "It's a story of hope."

It was? "Where?"

Her mouth flickered with a smirk. "Patience."

I'd never heard of that. Must have been a goblin thing.

On the fabric, the pretty pastoral scene was choked with white, lightning-veined fog. I went cold, remembering the feeling of it pressed up to me like a physical being, its laughter ringing in my ears. How many people here had faced the Haar and lived? Had the troupe themselves seen it?

The player in white continued somersaulting across the ground, his actions more and more menacing. I'd give him credit; it was creepy as hell. Definitely nailed the vibe of the Haar. I hugged my arms to my middle as the narrator went on, as the village on the canvas was blotted out entirely.

"The Haar has taken much, but will we let it take Lazankh from us?"

I was surprised by the cries of *No!* People were getting invested in the show; I watched them edge forward, eyes fixed on the players.

"No," the narrator King agreed passionately, flinging his hand for emphasis even as he held one side of the fabric. Light caught the gold mirrors sewn along the neckline of his tunic. "We will not. But who will fight the Haar? Who will save us?"

Sapphire light burst from a gem on the third performer's lapel, and I rolled my eyes skyward when I realised who this guy was meant to be. The long wavy hair should have given it away, or the look of self-importance on his face.

"The prince!" a kid shouted, others taking up the call as the vibrant Kier backflipped across the ground. Because of course. How else could you fight cannibalistic smoke?

Magic shimmered over the fabric and the scene now hung by itself as the king and the prince stepped away.

"Prince Kier! Prince Kier!"

Calanthe slanted a look in my direction and laughed at the look on my face.

"Do they really think he'll save them?" I asked quietly.

She nodded, something sad entering her brown eyes. "He can repel the fog; it runs from him. Only him, no one else." She shrugged, watching as the brightly coloured prince pirouetted past, throwing a splash of blue light at the Haar's white body.

"Will his highness save us from the Haar?" the King shouted, now standing off to the side of the floating village scene. Watching the theatrical battle between Haar and Kier.

I watched sceptically as light flashed between the prince and the Haar. I wasn't sure it was magic; more for show than anything real. But the crowd gasped as blue light flared brighter, and the Haar twisted and spun and dove to escape fake Kier.

"He'd never wear anything that bright," I said with a smirk, watching the choreographed fight. "I've only seen him in shades of black. Like his soul."

Oops, maybe I shouldn't have said that last part. But Calanthe laughed, thinking I wasn't serious. Or maybe thinking I was familiar enough with Kier to joke about him.

"He does seem to have a monochrome wardrobe," she whispered, as if someone would overhear. Was it treason to snark about a prince's clothes?

I jumped at the eruption of mist around the performers, the bright figure of the prince spinning and slashing at the Haar. The mist captured and enhanced the sapphire light until it was everywhere. I squinted, shielding my eyes with a hand and watching as the Haar's player let out a pitiful wail and fell dramatically to the ground.

The crowd cheered.

I raised a sceptical eyebrow. If Kier was able to end the Haar with his magic, he'd have done it by now. But his people clearly idolised him, and it made my stomach knot. When I got justice for Natasya's brutal murder, all these people would turn against me. They'd hunt me all across the goblin lands.

I clung to the idea of returning to Seagrave a legend who'd killed a goblin prince. The people here might hate me, but home I'd be a hero.

I forced myself to remember Natasya's body in cruel clarity, my determination sharpening as I brushed my fingers over the teardrops of my necklace—her necklace. He *deserved* to die.

Your prince can't save you, I wanted to tell these deluded people around me, but I kept my mouth shut. Not just because I didn't want to draw suspicion, but because most people hadn't noticed the princess in their midst yet, and I couldn't be bothered with all the attention.

I watched the performers take a bow, the painted fabric turning into a blank white sheet that fell to the ground, and I turned over what I'd learned. Not much, annoyingly. Hardly anything, actually. They thought Kier could end it, and it had started five years ago. This was a waste of time.

"We should go," Calanthe said, the urgency in her voice snapping my attention to her. "We shouldn't linger."

She'd been enthusiastic a minute ago; what had changed?

At my frown, she whispered, "It's supposed to be the king who saves us in the performance. But the king's actor stood by, watched, and did nothing. It's an insult at best, treason at worst."

I eyed the performers in a new light. Rebellious little fuckers. I turned to walk away, but something the king said rippled through my mind.

As if the death of our beloved princess hadn't hurt us enough, the Haar swallowed our villages the same week. Stole our people.

What were the chances of the princess dying and the Haar emerging in the same fucking week? The humans had done this somehow. I gnashed my teeth. My own damn people had nearly got me killed in Cyana.

"What an honour," a silken voice purred, colours flashing in front of me as I took a step, halting my path abruptly. The performer who'd played the king stood in front of me in his gaudy costume, a smirk on his deeply tanned face and mercury-silver eyes glimmering. "If I'd realised I had a royal audience, I would have put in more effort."

"Into doing nothing?" I asked dryly.

Calanthe tugged on my sleeve, a tense look on her freckled face. A black-clad guard closed in, eyes narrowed on the performer as he edged closer to me.

I lifted my head, chin high, ready to punch him in the dick if the fake king tried anything.

"There's so much power coming to life inside you, your highness," the actor said, silky and edged at the same time. "If you want to know how to use it properly, instead of the pretty power your advisers will teach you, come find the Troupe of Disaster."

I didn't tell him I didn't have advisers, that I'd been taught nothing, that I wasn't even acknowledging I could do magic. I just reached out and pinched his neck, pleased to find out the spot was a universal way of sending someone to their knees no matter their species.

"You're in my personal space," I said sweetly, just before my guard swept in with a face like thunder and a sword aimed for the fake king's throat.

"Just wishing her highness a happy marriage," the performer said with a genuine smile, bowing deeply when he got back to his feet. Well, the fucker was a good liar, I'd give him that.

"And you have. Now back off," the guard growled. He

was very good, very menacing. We should give him a pay rise.

The player bowed and joined the other two performers accepting coins from the crowd, ignoring their disapproving glares.

"Much appreciated," I told the guard, turning my back on the players but keeping my ears pricked just in case the fucker decided to stab me in the back. He seemed to be Kier's fan, but that shit about learning proper magic? Sketchy as hell. Intriguing—what did he mean by *real* magic?—but sketchy.

I caught the frown the guard sent my way. He wasn't one of the few who'd come with us to Cyana but I'd seen his face around.

"What?" I asked. "Not used to people saying thank you?"

His throat bobbed as he scanned the crowd, carving us a path through it. His pale face turned pink. He must have been older than forty, but he was blushing. "It's a rare day indeed, your highness."

I smirked. Well *someone* had a crush on me. Cute.

"Shall we head back to the castle?" Calanthe asked, still looking tense after the mini-treason the players had committed.

The smirk fell off my face; I tried not to drag my feet. Time for this fun day out to end; time to go back to the charade that I wasn't married to a man I imagined stabbing to death every hour of the day.

"It's almost time for dinner," she added.

Oh well, then. I was returning to a castle full of enemies who'd kill me if they discovered my plan. But at least there was food.

20

"*A*nd here I was thinking we were having a romantic night to ourselves," I drawled, strolling into the domed courtyard in the heart of the royal rooms. The sky was already turning rich blue above, the moon a pale sliver, but the grey walls and blue mosaic floor were lit by braziers burning bright aqua.

Kier sat in one of the low-slung chairs around the coffee table, Rook draped across the sofa opposite him and Xiona smirking from a chair as she sipped from a glass full of amber liquid.

I could have left them down here, found a staff member, and asked them to bring food to my room. But the rich scent of butter and spiced bread met my nose and my stomach growled.

Reminding myself not to be too *Letta*, I stalked across the glittering blue floor and grabbed the bottle of whiskey from the table, taking two long swallows. I didn't have to be the perfect princess but I had to seem harmless. No threats, no stabbing, no vicious grins.

But I wasn't going to make it to the goblin moon playing sweet little Zabaletta, even in front of his friends.

"Damn, brideling," Rook said with a laugh.

"Yeah, she's not as meek as she first seemed," Kier commented, drawling enough that I cast a look in his direction and smirked at the sheen covering his eyes.

"Can't handle your drink, dear husband?" I asked, claiming the only vacant seat; a chaise longue. I kicked off my boots and stretched out with a groan, nowhere near calm among these people but relieved to be off my feet.

Xiona cackled at my quip, long honey hair sliding over her shoulder as she turned her head to look at me. "You've grown fangs."

"Or maybe I had them all along," I replied, dampening the fierce grin that wanted to form on my face to something less sharp.

"Ooooh," Rook laughed.

Kier rolled his eyes, reaching for a glass and taking a long swallow. "Mother spare me."

"Aww, don't be a misery guts," Xiona chided, kicking his knee. "You're bringing the mood down, Kier."

"I'm devastated," he replied flatly, making me laugh.

I wished I could say I sat here to sneak information out of them, or to assess my enemy before I struck, but my whole motivation was the butter-smeared flatbread sitting on the table. I helped myself to a big piece, my eyes squeezing shut as garlic and spices burst across my tongue.

"Does she look like that when you go down on her, or is it just food that gives her that face?" Rook asked casually.

I choked on a laugh, forced myself to safely swallow my food, and slitted a glare in his direction. Kier was giving him the same narrow stare I was, a muscle feathering in his stubbled jaw.

I noticed that Kier didn't tell his friends we hadn't gotten sexual. Interesting. So he wanted us to seem like a real married couple to everyone but us? Fine by me; it'd make me less of a suspect when the 'rebels' killed him.

So I flashed Rook a sultry smile and said sweetly, "You mean you haven't heard me screaming every night? My husband is talented."

Kier coughed out a laugh, shooting me a surprised stare.

"Sorry," I stage-whispered. "Wasn't I supposed to tell them that?"

Something dark and hot lurked in Kier's eyes when he met my gaze, and I swallowed, my heart picking up.

"I believe it," Xiona remarked, ripping off a piece of bread and plopping it in her mouth. "That's the sexually charged stare of two people fucking like rabbits."

I groaned, breaking the stare. "Alright, that's enough commentary about my sex life." My non-existent sex life. "What are you two doing here?"

"Enriching your night with our presence?" Rook offered, a dazzling smile splitting his dark face.

"Cock-blocking you?" Xiona countered, flashing her teeth in a crooked smile.

"They came with news of the emergency village," Kier cut in, rolling dark blue eyes at his friends.

It struck me how normal this was, how this same scene was playing out in a hundred houses across goblin *and* human lands. They might have been princes and power players in this country, but they were just friends getting drunk and being dicks to each other.

"And?" I asked, eating more bread to cover up my discomfort at the ordinary, casual scene. I dipped it in spicy tomato sauce for good measure. Maybe it could burn all the feelings out of me.

"And there's enough houses for fifty people so far," Xiona told me, swirling the liquid in her glass. "It's a start."

"Kier tells us you came up with the idea, brideling," Rook said, snagging my attention. There was something disarmingly genuine in his smile, even with his eyes simmering and suggestive. He was as handsome and devastating as ever, but I had enough problems without having an affair with a goblin. Being married to one was bad enough.

I waved a hand, itchy at all their eyes on me. I preferred to blend into the shadows unless I was standing on the table of a salt-stained inn, singing a bawdy song off-key. "I have good ideas sometimes. Don't act so surprised."

Xiona smirked, draining her glass dry. "Sometimes."

I narrowed my eyes, licking the spicy sauce from my fingers and ignoring Kier's dark stare. "What's that supposed to mean?"

"You volunteered to marry a goblin to pause a war," Xiona drawled, flicking her hair over her other shoulder to give me a droll look. "I question your intelligence hourly."

"I did the same," Kier pointed out with a sulky look on his face. He propped his boots on the table, raking a hand distractingly through his long, wavy hair. I dragged my eyes away, fixed them on Xiona as she flashed a toothy grin.

"I question your intelligence by the minute, Kier."

He hissed. She batted her lashes.

I reached for more bread and ignored the canny look Rook aimed my way, as if he could tell I was uncomfortable.

Kier stretched, a strip of dark gold skin bared between his tight black shirt and his trousers, snagging my attention. Judging by the deep smirk on his face, he'd meant to draw my stare. Bastard.

Movement over his shoulder caught my attention instead, and I narrowed my eyes as the silver surface of a black-framed mirror rippled. I half expected it to start playing an opera—the magic in this castle was crazy and outrageous—but when a shoulder pushed through, as if through a sheet of water, I jumped to my feet, reaching for the knife in my sleeve.

"Easy," Kier said, suddenly beside me with soft blue eyes and a deeply amused smile. "It's not the rebels, you're safe here."

I didn't take my eyes off the mirror as a small-framed woman pushed through, dressed in black from head to toe. It took me a moment to realise there were black scales flowing from the leather armour at her shoulders, down to the gauntlets at her wrists. I let out a hissed breath through clenched teeth, relaxing increment by increment. She was one of his guards, not a threat.

An arm slung over my shoulder, and I slanted a glare at Rook as he tucked me into a hug, grinning.

"Fierce bridling. Were you leaping to our defence?"

"To my own," I corrected, narrowing my eyes further. "I see you've chosen your cause of death. I wouldn't have picked provoking me into stabbing you for touching me, but you do you, Rook."

Xiona barked a loud laugh, grinning at me. "I didn't know humans could be this interesting."

"I didn't know goblins could be this maddeningly normal," I fired back, extricating myself from Rook.

He went and threw his arm around Xiona instead, seemingly content despite the warning look she gave him.

"Odele," Kier greeted, nodding at the guard who stopped a few feet from the chairs and sofas, hands clasped behind her back. "I'm guessing you have something to tell us since you've come all this way."

Odele nodded abruptly, her expression so fierce and

intense that I didn't let my guard down. Her face was flushed, the same deeply tanned shade as Kier, and her intense dark eyes swept over each of us, lingering on me. I didn't offer any explanation for my presence; everyone knew Kier had a human bride. If she couldn't put two and two together, she was an idiot.

"The border's active again," she said, dismissing me and facing Kier, her chin high and her face full of grave importance. I immediately disliked her. "Greenheart's amassing an army to test our security."

Greenheart was amassing an army? As in, the other goblin court? Great, that was just what we fucking needed. A war on two fronts—three if you counted the Haar. I needed to get the hell out of this place the second the goblin moon rose.

"How big?" Xiona asked, stalking forward, her brow pinched. "And what kind of weaponry are we talking? Don't tell me they've rolled out those massive emerald cannons."

"Not yet," Odele replied, haughty and self-important. She flicked a long, black braid over her shoulder, less sass in the gesture than Xiona's hair flick. "But each one is armed with a crystal-tipped spear, and gem-reinforced shielding."

"Great," Kier growled, crossing his arms over his chest.

"And I passed by Skayan on the way here," Odele added, with an air of expectation. "Rumours swirl in the capital about your brothers, sire."

My gaze went flat at her simpering *sire*. No one else called him that. She sounded ridiculous.

"What rumours?" Kier asked intently, angling himself towards her.

"If the whispers are to be believed—"

I rolled my eyes. *The whispers.* So mysterious.

Rook grinned at me, his pearly teeth sharp and eyes glimmering. "Feeling possessive, brideling?" he whispered.

I gave him the middle finger, to his utter delight.

"—your brothers angle for the throne," Odele finished, with an expectant look at Kier.

"Not particularly surprising," Xiona commented, watching her friend. "What else did you hear in Skayan?" she asked Odele, the guard's—spy's?—mouth thinning.

"That is all," Odele replied, clearly not happy about it. I narrowed my eyes. I got the sense Xiona was pretty high ranking, and Rook, too. The blatant disrespect didn't seem to piss off Xiona, but it would have made me stabby.

"Thank you, Odele," Kier said with a dismissive nod. I was more than pleased to watch a flicker of frustration move through her brown eyes.

She turned, and paused. I narrowed my eyes, watching her face us again. "Oh, but I did see the Haar on my way here. It's taken Icana and Ocel."

Two more villages—or were these towns? Cities?

"You say that so casually," I said, barely leashing my anger. It pissed me off that she'd timed that bombshell for dramatic effect and attention, and it pissed me off that there was no ounce of care in her voice. Two villages would mean *hundreds* dead. Kids like Ari, cowering and whimpering as the Haar swept in.

Odele straightened, her mouth tightening just slightly on the edges. She didn't like me; fine, I didn't like her, either.

I tilted my head, watching her. "They're your people; don't you care that the Haar has swallowed their homes at best, and murdered them at worst?"

Odele's eyes slid up and down my body, full of judgement.

Before I could even return the gesture Xiona let out a

low, rumbling laugh. "Bold of you to look that way at a princess, Odele. You're a braver woman than me, especially considering our prince seems smitten with his new wife."

With a crooked grin, Xiona stalked back to her sofa and sprawled across it, refilling her glass.

"Thank you for your report, Odele," Kier said, cutting the tension. It was pretty fucking interesting that Xiona was on my side, even Rook edging closer in a clear signal of solidarity. Because I was his friend's wife, and part of their inner circle by default? "I'll get the finer details from you later."

Of all things, Odele shot me a victorious look. I rolled my eyes. If she wanted Kier, she could have him. Until the goblin moon, at least.

I watched the guard step through the liquid mirror, the rippling magic stilling, and then glared at my husband. "So much for us being the only people who can come here."

Kier turned to me, "The mirror is for my most elite team. Only three people know of it."

"And you picked the biggest assholes for that honour?" Xiona drawled. "Don't even *think* about it," she added to Rook as he sauntered over to her.

"They're good at their jobs," Kier argued, ignoring Rook as he splayed himself over Xiona, running a hand through her long, honey hair. "It doesn't matter if they're assholes."

"Ha!" Xiona crowed, pushing aside Rook's face with the flat of her palm when he tried to kiss her cheek. "So you admit they're assholes."

Kier rolled his eyes, looking to me, as if *I* was the voice of reason.

I shrugged. "I think Odele's a dick, too. Also, I'm done here. I only came for your food."

"Aww, don't go, brideling," Rook complained, lifting his dark head from Xiona's shoulder.

"Sorry to break your heart," I said with zero sincerity, heading for the stairs to the upstairs level.

"I'll find you later," Kier murmured, watching me leave.

He wouldn't, but it kept our cover intact. "I'll wait with bated breath," I purred, ignoring the way his eyes darkened, something dangerous gleaming in their depths.

I was playing a deadly game, and not simply because I was here to kill him. I was his *wife*—and if Kier decided to call my bluff, I knew I would lose.

21

"**S**on of a bitch," I hissed, digging my fingernails into the mortar holding together the bricks of my balcony window. A week had passed with nothing to do, no tours of the city or rebel attacks or even the princess duties I'd expected to be dumped on me. I'd been left to my own devices, little more than a decorative bit of furniture, and I was *bored*.

Plus, I needed my own supply of fog's ruin just in case I encountered the Haar on my escape from the goblin lands.

Three weeks to go, and then I was out of here.

"Shit," I hissed when the toe of my boot slipped from where I'd wedged it between bricks. I missed my rubber shoes so damn badly. Missed my gloves, too; my fingers were already raw at the tips, my palms scraped and fingernails ragged. But if that was the price of exploring this city by myself, so be it.

Breath hissed through my clenched teeth as I held onto the wall by sheer stubbornness and grit. I fumbled for somewhere more stable to balance my boot, hanging there for a second to catch my breath before I began to climb down. It was lucky I'd spent years scaling buildings in Seagrave, or I'd never have made this descent.

But it felt good to be doing something, to not be shut in my room or sprawled across the sofa in the courtyard waiting for something interesting to happen. With Calanthe at my side, I'd toured the castle twice from top to bottom, but there were only so many mirrors and marble busts I could look at before it became dull. Even the secret doors had lost their sheen of curiosity, even if I made a mental note of where each led to.

I had my escape route planned, had imagined a hundred different ways I'd finally confront Kier about Natasya's death, but the waiting was *killing* me. If I attacked him now, he'd survive. Fucking goblin royalty and their invulnerability.

"Thank fuck," I grunted when I finally landed on the ground, grass softening the final drop from a windowsill. The bag slung around my body smacked my thigh as I fought to steady my balance.

I batted a strand of auburn hair from my face and scanned the grassy space between me and the castle wall. Empty of guards, though I doubted they were far away. I stepped into a shadow and followed it, flattening myself to a rounded tower wall with a hiss when footsteps crunched the grass.

Hairs rose along the back of my neck as they neared, and I seriously hoped my dark leggings and long-sleeved shirt would camouflage me in the darkness. A soft wind moved through my ponytail, and I fought a shiver, praying it didn't carry my scent to the person getting closer with every footstep.

Thanks to my daily chats with Calanthe, I knew goblins

had higher senses of smell and sight than humans, but would it be acute enough to pinpoint where I hid?

I held my breath as the figure rounded the corner, tall and broad but slumped like they were bored of doing the rounds. Perfect. Boredom equaled sloppiness, and guards' sloppiness was my best friend.

I watched the figure's every movement, braced for them to snap their gaze towards me, but they slouched past my hiding place and continued onwards. I let out a slow breath.

I wasn't doing anything illegal—everyone and their aunt had a vial of fog's ruin around here despite how rare Rook had made it seem at first—but sneaking around at night looked suspicious as hell.

I could have asked Calanthe for a steady supply of vials, but I wanted to dodge the questions thrown my way. Why would I need fog's ruin when I had a fog-repelling husband?

I waited for the guard to carry on around another corner, and walked steadily toward the high wall. While I was out, I could take a look around Lakankh anyway, see the parts my guards didn't want me to.

My heart rate picked up with exhilaration and excitement as I climbed over the wall and jumped down on the other side. I swiftly blended into the shadows when a man glanced my way, mumbling to himself but clearly seven cups deep. I smirked when he walked face-first into a street light. No worry of him remembering the princess climbing over the castle walls; or of anyone believing him if he *did* remember.

"Oh, I love that one!" I whispered to myself as he started up a very vulgar song. Huh. So goblins and humans had the same ballads?

A smile crept across my face as I headed in the opposite direction to the man, eyeing the curtain of blue trees draped across the mountains on the east side. Silversweet grew in the darkest shade; if I was going to find it anywhere, it was there.

Suppressing a sigh at the trek ahead and wondering why I didn't just pull rank as a princess, I set off across the city, keeping my ears peeled for any gossip or useful tidbits of information.

C

I OVERHEARD NOTHING USEFUL, except a hasty, very questionable deal being agreed upon in an alleyway, and a formidable woman called Beryn soundly slapping her sister across the face for having an affair with her husband.

By the time I rolled back over the castle walls and dropped down on the inside, sweat stuck my clothes to my skin and I was ready to crawl into bed and sleep until dawn.

There'd been enough silversweet in the forest to fill an orangery, perfuming the trees with its sweet scent. I'd filled my bag to the brim, picking up a few other herbs along the way. Less the kind used to season a broth than the kind that would knock someone out for a few hours, make them choke on their own spit, or bleed from their eyeballs.

It was a worthwhile trip, and I was feeling almost optimistic as I flattened myself to the wall, waiting for a guard to pass, and then started up the tower to my balcony. All I needed was syrup, and I had enough fog's ruin to get through miles of Haar on the way out of the goblin lands.

Two weeks to go; I was ready.

A sharp pang moved through my chest at the thought of walking away when the fog was swallowing villages and eating people, Ari's indigo face flashing behind my eyes. They'd be fine. There was a temporary town set up for them, and Kier actually seemed to give a shit about helping them. Why else would he race to Cyana to help?

But Kier would be dead, an annoying voice reminded me. *You'd be leaving them defenceless.*

"Only as defenceless as Natasya was when he ripped her apart," I hissed at myself, digging my fingernails between bricks to haul myself up, the muscles of my arms burning in protest.

I gritted my teeth and focused on the climb to shut out my thoughts. There was only the brick, my fingertips, and the sweat dripping from my forehead. My heart pounded the further I climbed, the exertion clearing my head even if it exhausted my already tired body.

"Almost there," I panted. "And then you can sleep for a year."

I hadn't considered the climb back up when I'd planned this night-time excursion. Never fucking again.

I groaned in relief when I closed my hand around a curvaceous column of the balcony. I hauled myself up by the smooth stone, flopping ungracefully onto the balcony with a rough sound of relief.

I let my eyes flutter shut, just for a second, just to recover my strength.

They flew open again at the gravelly voice that said, "So nice of you to finally come home, wife.

22

*S*hit. Holy. Burning. Shit.

"Ugh," I groaned, my body too achy to do much more than jolt in surprise when Kier pushed off the flat wall beside my bedroom door.

"Where on Mother's earth have you been?" he demanded, glaring down at me and looking too damn hot with his white shirt and long hair all dishevelled.

I rolled onto my front and pushed to my feet, groaning when my arms and legs throbbed.

"Out," I panted, meeting his furious gaze and swallowing when he backed me up against the wall, his face like thunder.

"More specific than out," Kier said through gritted teeth, caging me with his arms and looking half inclined to kill me. Or more than half.

I rolled my eyes skyward, not seeing another way out except to tell the truth. Besides, picking silversweet wasn't illegal. What was he gonna do? Forbid me from going flower picking?

"Fine," I muttered, starting to catch my breath after the climb. "I went to get *this*, okay?"

I very carefully pulled out only the silversweet, not the more exciting poisonous stuff, and waved it in my dear husband's face. "I never want to be at the mercy of that fucking fog again."

Truth—a hundred percent truth. It's why I refused to have an escape plan without a way to subdue the Haar.

Kier blinked dark eyes at me, surprise in the slackening of his tanned face.

"Satisfied?" I bit out, glaring at him and not even trying to hide how much I hated him.

"There's a store of silversweet in the basement of the castle," he rumbled, head tilted as he considered me. "You could have asked for it at any time."

"*Wow*," I said with so much fake bullshit it practically dripped sarcasm. "You're so right, I should *definitely* have asked for silversweet from the store I didn't know *existed*. Great idea, why didn't I think of that?"

Kier didn't back off, but the unforgiving line of his mouth softened just slightly. "Nobody told you about it?"

"Nobody tells me *anything!*" I expelled a hard breath, wondering if he could really be this stupid. "You married me, brought me here, and cloistered me in your damn castle where I'm supposed to be a princess but I'm treated like a child."

I rolled my eyes at his shock. "No, nobody told me about the store of silversweet. Who *would* tell me—you? You can't stand the sight of me, which is fair enough, I hate all your kind, too. But you can't expect me to magically know things. The world doesn't work like that."

I shoved the plant back in my bag, pissed as hell and a tiny bit embarrassed. Okay, a lot embarrassed. I was an assassin and a thief, and I'd been caught sneaking into my own room. Amateur.

"Can I enter my own damn room now?" I demanded, glaring up at my hateful husband.

But his attention had dropped to my bag—no, to my arm I realised with a jolt of alarm when his hand snared my wrist.

"What," he asked slowly, "is this?"

He peeled up my sleeve to reveal the knife I had strapped there. Shit. Not fucking good.

"Ah," I said. That was all I had—*ah*. I licked my lip, swallowing. I could talk my way out of this—I could. Except I couldn't think of anything.

While Kier was focused on the dagger sheathed on my wrist—a strange mix of emotions chasing through his eyes —I made a quick grab for the knife strapped up my spine beneath my shirt.

I had it pressed to Kier's throat in a second, breathing fast, goosebumps breaking out all across my body.

I couldn't kill him, but I could make him bleed. I could draw his blood and cut him up the same way he'd done to Natasya. I could make him *pay*.

"Who are you?" he breathed, watching me with slitted eyes. His throat moved against my knife, drawing a thin trickle of blood, and my own blood sang with satisfaction.

"You know who I am," I growled. "Zabaletta Stellara. Your wife. Your damn princess now, although princess of *what* I have no fucking clue."

Offhand, I added, "I might not be as sweet and harmless as previously advertised."

Kier laughed—fucking *laughed*. It was a low, dangerous sound that sent a shiver through me.

"I didn't bother to come to your room before tonight,"

Kier said, voice rough as he watched me, breathing shallowly. "But I figured we should make *some* attempt to be a real husband and wife, since the marriage appears to be holding a ceasefire. For now."

I raised an eyebrow. His point was...?

"I didn't come before now because you bored me," he went on, his heavy stare trailing from my glaring eyes past my clenched jaw to my body. "Especially in the beginning, when you were *sweet and harmless* as you say. When you began to speak your mind, showing an actual personality, I hoped there might be something salvageable in this marriage. But still—"

He shrugged, thumb pressing to the rapid pulse in my wrist. "I knew beneath all your sharpness, there was a soft heart. A weak mind."

I snorted. I definitely deserved an award for best actress. I pressed my knife harder into Kier's neck, my heart hammering when he responded by sliding his hand up my arm, clasping my own throat.

"You no longer bore me, Zabaletta Kollastus," Kier said, and kissed me.

I jerked back, my head hitting the wall, but Kier flexed his hand on my throat and kissed me harder. I couldn't ignore the tremor that moved through me, or the thrill that curled in my lower belly. I couldn't stop my groan, or my rush of poisonous satisfaction as I kissed him back, every crush of lips and battle of teeth a declaration: *I hate you, I want you, I hate you.*

Kier groaned and dragged me closer by his hand on my neck, angling his mouth for a deeper kiss. I hated myself even as I opened for his tongue, even as his taste drugged me, even as my head spun and I lost myself.

His body was hard and powerful against mine, the

muscle of his chest burning hot and heaving with frantic breaths. I hated that I loved feeling it against me, hated that I slid my left hand over his chest and down his abs to feel even more.

A knot unwound in my chest, air filling lungs that had been tight for weeks even as Kier kissed me breathless. He didn't care about the steady drip of blood into his collar, utterly mindless as he kissed me.

It was merciless. Endless. I was a country he conquered with every bruising kiss, and for a second I was desperate to surrender.

Cold doused me when blue light flashed between us, and I jumped back, the sharp blade leaving Kier's gold throat as magic flickered from the ring on my hand.

"Shit," I rasped, panic at what was happening, at what I'd just *done*, robbing me of whatever breath I'd managed to choke down. Robbing me of any peace of mind I'd managed to claim while I was in the woods.

Kier's lapel erupted with an answering light, the sapphire brooch pinned there sputtering to life, and he swore, stepping away to rake a hand through his messy black hair.

"So it's true," he muttered, and shot me an unreadable look. Was he suspicious? Horrified? Turned on? "You're my mate—and I'm yours. That's why our magic reacted like that."

Ice moved through me as Kier took another step back, shaking his head. "This wasn't supposed to happen."

"You're telling *me*," I snarled, lowering my dagger, my hand shaky.

I'd kissed him—and enjoyed it. My sister's murderer.

"Kiss me again, and I'll kill you," I threatened, and swallowed hard when Kier's eyes flared with obvious arousal.

The psycho liked when I threatened him? Well, he'd *love* it when I buried my knife in his throat on the goblin moon.

"Do it," he taunted, his voice slipping deeper as he stalked back to me, grabbing my chin while I was too stunned to stab him.

He lowered his head, holding me in place while he sucked my lower lip into his mouth, tongue running along it and making my whole body tighten.

"I'll enjoy every minute," he promised, gravelly and carnal.

Shit. I was in big, big trouble, and I didn't know how to get out. I'd have preferred him throwing me into a dungeon for sneaking out to the molten heat pouring through my veins.

"Something tells me you'll enjoy it too, mate," he added, sucking a spot on my neck that made me limp before stepping back, looking mightily pleased with himself.

That was the problem. I couldn't enjoy *any* of it. Not a single moment. I had to keep my head straight, and my focus where it should be: murder. Not begging my husband to fuck my brains out against the wall.

"Try me," I replied, teeth bared as I fumbled the door open and vanished inside, leaving him out on the balcony and praying he didn't call my bluff.

23

*E*ight boring days and sleepless nights later, I woke to the disorienting feeling of a weight across my middle and delicious heat cradling my back.

Languid with sleep, I relaxed into the comfort of being held, let the warmth seep into my bones as my eyes fluttered —and I realised someone was in bed with me.

I reached for the knife under my pillow and came up empty.

"How many knives do you actually have?" asked my husband's unmistakable voice, unusually scratchy. Had he slept here beside me? Had he just woken up, too?

I narrowed my eyes as I turned over, reminding myself to be sweet because he got bored of it easily but unable to hold back my ire.

"Enough to cut your dick off before you can blink," I replied, raspy and rough. Ugh, this was the last thing I needed first thing in the morning.

Kier rolled onto his back, smirking as he toyed with the dagger I'd hidden under my pillow. I ignored the cold that flooded my back where we'd been pressed together.

"You look like shit," I told him, throwing back the covers and crossing the room to where I'd stashed a small throwing knife in the wardrobe. Also gone. *And* the ones under the chest of drawers, beneath the mattress, bundled among my underwear, and in my boot. Bastard.

Kier looked like the entitled prince he was, sprawled in my bed with the covers draped around his waist, dark gold chest bared and horrifically alluring. The sculpted muscle I'd felt when we kissed was on full display, and it took all my willpower not to stare. I hated him; he was a killer; he'd mutilated my sister.

That cleared my head enough to look at him objectively, scanning for weaknesses. He really did look like shit, with dark circles around his eyes and his hair rumpled and wayward, tiredness written in the lines of his stubbled face. So he hadn't slept with me all night; his voice was rough with exhaustion, not fresh sleep. Good.

"I was too busy to sleep," he replied with a shrug, watching me as he idly spun my dagger. Arrogant, indolent.

"Glad you're making healthy life choices," I said sarcastically, stalking over to him and ignoring his gaze as it poured over the transparent slip I'd slept in, eyes turning smoky with desire. "Give me my fucking knives."

"So you can stab me? I think not."

I crossed my arms over my chest, temper sparking hot. I only succeeded in drawing his attention to the low V of my neckline. "If I wanted to stab you, I'd have done it by now. I've had plenty of opportunities."

Kier made a low hum of agreement, tilting his head back as I stormed over to the bed. "I think I might enjoy being stabbed by you," he replied with a smirk.

"Are you insane?" I asked, shaking my head.

"Possibly," he agreed, arching his neck to look at me as I paused beside the bed, fuming.

I feinted a swipe with my right hand and grabbed for the dagger with my left, but he evaded both attempts with a laugh. I jumped hard as a hot hand slid over my thigh, the thin silk of my slip barely a barrier.

My skin tingled, heat rupturing through my body—and in my traitorous core.

But fine, if he wanted to touch me, I'd use it against him. I told myself it was entirely to arm myself with my knives again as I climbed onto the bed and swung a leg over him.

Kier let out an unexpected rumble as I settled on his lap, the covers between us doing nothing to hide his hardness. His eyelids dropped lower, his eyes sultry slits as he looked at me, making my whole body crawl with heat and the need to be touched.

I snatched my dagger from his hand, and wasn't sure I entirely won as his fingers glided up my back instead, mapping the bumps of my spine with a searing palm.

"Give me the rest of my knives," I hissed, my pulse racing in my throat as I glared at him, my whole body straining, aching.

"Mm." Kier's head ducked, lips dragging up my neck and making my eyes slam shut before I dragged them open again. Gods dammit, that felt too fucking good. When his tongue swirled over my weak spot, I was done for.

"Kiss me, and I will," he bargained.

"No," I protested weakly, on fire as he explored my body in luxurious, gliding strokes. He was drugging me with need again, muddying my mind like he had on the balcony, and like a masochist I let him, greedy for more.

"No kisses then," he agreed against my throat, my breath coming faster when he scraped his teeth over my skin.

Alarm and lust tangled up, and I couldn't separate the two. My skin buzzed where his hands slid down my arms and back up my sides, lingering over my ribs, thumbs caressing the underside of my boobs and making my stomach explode with nervous wings.

Shit, I needed to end this, to push his hands away, climb off, possibly launch myself from the balcony and hope I saw sense in the moment before I landed in the grass. I'd gone mad.

"If you want your knives," Kier said, thick with the same disgusting desire I felt, "touch me."

I hated him with all my heart, but I'd never hated anyone more than I hated myself for wanting to touch him. My palms itched where they hung at my sides, painfully aware of the bare skin of his chest so damn close.

The tiniest smirk lurked in the corner of his mouth as he drew back and met my dark stare, fingers getting bolder as they lingered on the sides of my breasts.

I swallowed hard, especially as Kier set his mouth to my ear and whispered, "Do you throb for me, Zaba?"

Gods. *No*. Fuck. *Yes*. I hated him, hated me, hated everything except the heat licking across my body, the touch making me feel so damn good.

"You're delusional," I managed to rasp.

"I think," he replied, thumbs making slow, excruciating circles over my nipples, "you want me so badly you can't think straight. I think if I slid my fingers under this silk, I'd find you soaked."

I shook so hard with restraint, wanting to grab his despicable face and kiss him until he bled.

A sharp rap on the door had me shooting away from him, jumping off the bed like a panicked cat, my breathing wrecked and fast.

He killed your sister, I hissed at myself in the safety of my own mind. *He killed your sister, he killed your fucking sister.*

"Come in," Kier growled to whoever had knocked, despite this being *my* damn room. "This had better be good, Jocaste," he growled at the deeply blue woman who stood stiffly in the doorway, dark horns jutting upward from her brow and her fangs so long they hung over her bottom lip.

"There's a messenger for you, your highness," Jocaste said, so professional, she didn't glance at where I shook in front of the window or at Kier's heaving chest.

"Tell them to *wait*."

"From the capital, your highness," Jocaste elaborated, not betraying a single emotion. Impressive. I could have used some of her coolness right now; I was hot and breathless and seething with shame. "He requested an audience with you and her highness."

Don't bring me into it, I groaned internally.

Kier heaved a sigh and nodded to the messenger's messenger. "Thank you, Jocaste. Tell them I'll be there in an hour."

"They requested to speak to you immediately," she said, tone carefully neutral.

"Tell them I'll see them in an hour," Kier reiterated.

Jocaste nodded, bowed her head, and closed the door behind herself.

Kier glared at the ceiling, one side of his lips curled back, baring pearly teeth. "Come here."

"In your fucking dreams," I laughed shortly.

His eyes dragged slowly to me, darkness and hate simmering there. "This meeting is going to be a nightmare for both of us. Let's feel good for a few minutes before it."

I raised an eyebrow in judgement, crossing my arms over my chest and ignoring the deep throb in my core at what he proposed. "That's all you can manage? Some husband you are."

His churning hatred turned to molten want, and a chill rushed down my spine. "If only we had time for me to show you just how long I can make you scream, mate."

My hand flexed at my side; I wanted to run it through my hair and pull at the roots, but I suppressed the motion.

"We might not have long," he added, watching me intently, "but I can promise it will be good enough to melt your mind."

Holy shit.

"Okay, enough," I said, breathy as hell. "This isn't happening, so stop trying to seduce me."

"Why?" He grinned crookedly, hot as hell. I pointed my dagger at him. "Because it's working?"

Yes. Ugh. He looked so damn good, I wanted to scream.

"Get out of my bed," I ordered, turning my back on him and opening my wardrobe doors. "And put my knives back where you found them."

I set my single dagger down and pulled out a dark red dress with a killer neckline, the bodice heavily beaded.

"Fine," Kier agreed. I hissed when he was suddenly behind me, sweeping long hair off my shoulder to place a kiss there. "But we need to talk before you meet the messenger. We need to provide a united front, show no weaknesses. We hide our hate, at least until they're gone, and play the happily married couple."

I gasped. "You mean we're *not* a happily married couple?"

Kier pinched my side, and I snorted, killing my smile the second I felt it tugging at my cheeks.

"Fine," I agreed. "I'll pretend to be your doting wife. But there better be something in it for me."

"Not having my brothers and the rest of the capital's

denizens coming sniffing around here?" he offered, standing so close he was practically touching me.

"I doubt they could be worse than you," I muttered, trying not to wrinkle the fine velvet of the dress as his hands curled into fists.

"They hunt humans for sport, and make a game of coming up with new, inventive ways to torture people. Exactly," he said when I stiffened. "You'd never be safe with them."

Oh, so I'm safe with you? I wanted to snap.

I shrugged. "I'll take my chances," I replied offhandedly, pulling away from him and giving him a pointed look, lifting the dress. He needed to leave so I could wash and get dressed.

"They'll tear you to pieces," he said seriously, his body bristling in the corner of my eye. "They'll do it just because you're my wife. And then I'll be forced to recreate any wound dealt to your body tenfold on theirs."

I narrowed my eyes, meeting his violent glare head-on. "Wouldn't life be easier for you with me gone?" Why avenge me? Why give a shit?"

"I told you," he huffed. "If you're killed, it will destroy the ceasefire I got married for.

"Besides," he added, taking a step and reappearing in front of me with a flash of blue magic from one of his rings.

I recoiled when his fingers slid along my face, sinking into my hair to tilt my head back. I met his eyes with a narrowed glare.

"You fascinate me," he finished, low enough that the words shivered along my skin. "I want to know every bit of cleverness in your mind, and why you have so many knives. I want to feel the bite of one on my throat as you ride us both into oblivion."

I forgot how to breathe.

"And if someone takes you from me before I can do that," he said, voice even lower, "*I'll rip them to shreds.*"

My heart hammered. I swallowed. "Good to know," I said weakly. "Now get out; I need to dress."

Kier made my sanity unravel by kissing my temple before backing off and hunting for his shirt. It was a simple kiss, chaste and casual, and I shook so hard the beads on the velvet dress rattled before I stilled my hands.

"Remember what I said—we need to pretend to be enamoured with each other," he said, dragging a black shirt over his head and tugging it into place. "If this messenger senses *any* weakness, an envoy will come, and I can guarantee one of my brothers will be among it. If you want a relatively normal life, play along today. Save thoughts of stabbing me for later," he added with a sharp grin.

The fucking psycho. He liked all my sharpness, my knives, my ... me. He liked *me*, abrasive and threatening and prickly.

What the hell was I supposed to do with *that* knowledge?

"I'll play along," I agreed distractedly, barely paying attention as Kier headed for the door.

"Meet me downstairs; I'll have breakfast brought to the courtyard."

"Yeah," I murmured, holding the dress to my chest like it was armour. Like it could protect me from my realisation.

Kier liking me would make it easier to kill him when the goblin moon fell, I told myself. But it left a sick taste in my mouth.

24

*T*he beaded train of the deep red dress rustled behind me as I walked side by side with Kier, down a narrow hallway accessible only to the two of us and his guards.

"Let me do the talking," he said for the third time, visibly nervous as he spoke to me in a low voice. "The last thing we want is you drawing attention."

"Only speak when I'm spoken to," I replied sweetly, batting my lashes. "Got it, husband."

"*Please* no sass," he groaned, pinching the bridge of his nose.

"Show no personality," I agreed with a sage nod.

"Mother save me," he whispered with an upward glance. And then launched right back into his rules with, "Stay a step behind me—"

"Live in your shadow—"

"And don't react to anything the messenger says to provoke you."

I shot him a frown, my dress dragging along the floor.

Velvet and beading was pretty, but *damn*, it was heavy. "Why would they want to provoke me?"

"To insult me. To insult you. To get a rise out of you, and undermine my rule here." He listed them without much thought, as if this was something he obsessed over. As if he'd been waiting for someone to come snoop at our marriage.

"Undermine your rule," I echoed, glancing at Kier sideways as the hallway seemed to stretch endlessly ahead of us, panelled wood as far as I could see. "There are people who don't want you here, aren't there? In Lazank, in the castle."

Kier nodded, a muscle feathering in his square jaw. "Many."

"And if you get kicked out of Lazank, I'd be exiled with you," I mused. "Or kept here as some kind of pet for your usurper."

"Or killed before you can even flee," he countered, tenser with every word.

"We'd better not let that happen, then, dear husband," I decided, sliding my hand into his and satisfied by his jolt of surprise. I gave him a sweet smile that should have won awards and watched the play of admiration on his face. "I'll help you convince the messenger we're a happy family, and you can reward me for my efforts."

His sapphire eyes darkened.

"I'm sure you have royal coffers somewhere," I added. "Or even better: a vault. I want another dagger."

A laugh burst from him, making his eyes glimmer and a damned *dimple* appear in his cheek. "How about a sword?"

Butterflies spun through my belly, and he nodded at whatever he saw on my face.

"A sword for my mate, then. I know just the one."

If that wasn't a good incentive to act my way through this meeting, I didn't know what was.

I batted my eyelashes at Kier and said in a honeyed, breathy voice, "You're too good to me, Kier."

"Save that voice," he replied, eyes even darker. "I want you to use it later when I give you your real reward."

Cold raced down my back, even as heat curled through my lower belly. I was more than grateful when the silent guard ahead of us stopped in front of a small, oak door set in the wall.

Time to put on a show. This was getting its own chapter in my bestselling memoir.

25

*K*ier hissed under his breath as the guard opened the small door and we glided through, regal and straight-backed. I acted my ass off, not channeling Orchid this time but Celandrine.

"Problem?" I whispered, my expression somewhere between curious and sweet as we walked into a tall, intimidating space dominated by a high-backed throne made entirely of lapis spikes. Beside it, a smaller throne glimmered, sky blue crystal and completely transparent.

I let my eyes slide over the small retinue of people waiting in the middle of the long room and the much bigger collective of black-scaled guards and gold-liveried staff. If I were Kier, I'd have hidden some guards among the staff, too. Our guests were decked in more beading, embroidery, fringing, and ornamentation than I'd ever seen in my life, jewels and gems stitched along their collars and gleaming with magic. A show of strength, then.

"Allenon, the one in the middle," Kier murmured out of the side of his mouth, keeping his hand in mine as we approached the set of thrones, heads held high. I kinda liked Kier like this, in full badass mode, turned against enemies other than me. "He must be the messenger who summoned me. He's the king's chief adviser, and his lover. Don't underestimate him. And don't tell him anything."

"Like what?" I whispered, barely moving my lips as I offered a smile to every damn person watching us approach. The phrase *kill them with kindness* was very appealing right now.

I eyed the middle messenger, from his glossy silver hair to his sharp jaw, straight nose, and thin mouth. He stood ruler-straight, and he must have been in his forties but I didn't see a single line on his fair skin. That more than anything told me just how rich the bastard was.

"Not a single thing," Kier reiterated, guiding me to my throne and holding my hand until I was situated, my skirts arranged neatly. He kissed the back of my hand and sat upon his own, much taller throne. He was probably compensating for a tiny bulge. I didn't need a big, showy throne; my metaphorical balls were bigger than his.

"Allenon," Kier finally greeted, leaning back against his brilliantly blue throne with his head cocked at an arrogant angle and his hands resting on the solid lapis arms. "I wasn't expecting you to visit. Thank you for coming, I know your schedule is extremely stretched."

Kier Kollastus! The sheer amount of sneering suggestion in those two final words made my mask almost slip. That little fucker. He'd told *me* not to say anything, and then taunted our visitor.

Allenon's shrewd eyes narrowed as he stepped forward and dipped his silver head in a pseudo-bow. "Your highness. I was already on my way to offer the king's blessing to you and your new wife—"

At this, Kier threw a blinding grin my way. I ducked my

head, hiding a coquettish smile and wishing I could blush on command.

"But my visit is more important now than ever," Allenon went on, a tightness around his eyes that hadn't been there before. "Skyan is buried under the fog."

Shit. The capital?

"And," the messenger continued, looking supremely pissed off, "there are only three cities remaining. One of which is yours."

"You're asking for aid," Kier supposed.

"I'm asking you to *end this*," Allenon disagreed, his tone biting. He stepped forward, a sneer curling his thin upper lip. "You're the only one who stands to gain anything. The two city governors have no direct line to the throne, but you —when the Haar devours your brothers and father, the Bluescale Court will be yours."

"And who says I want it?" Kier asked coolly, his stubbled face giving nothing away. "You presume a great deal, Allenon. I'll send aid, and as many people as I can spare to help evacuate survivors. The new town of Serul is growing every day, with homes for any refugees who can reach it."

A tremor of pride shot through me at that. My suggestion, and Kier's willingness to listen had done that. I could do real good here, I realised, and felt like a steaming pile of shit for what I planned. Nothing could sway me from my goal. Not even this.

"Cut the bullshit," Allenon said, stalking forward with a pinched expression on his poreless face.

I lifted my chin, watching, forcing myself to remember the role I had to play here. I couldn't shoot daggers at him, couldn't bare my teeth. If this bastard dragged the capital here, I'd be imprisoned at best, and I certainly wouldn't have revenge for Natasya's death. They'd steal that from me. Even if the place was buried under fog, this fucker had got out somehow. My money was on the royals escaping to safety, too.

"I know you did this," Allenon said with an ugly scrunch in his nose, light dancing through the gems sewn into his collar. "*Undo* it. Or you'll regret it."

Kier stiffened, fingernails carving into the arms of his lapis throne. No—shit—those were black claws at the tips of his fingers. A shudder slid down my back and I glanced quickly away. He could just call those things up at any time? Or was it only when he lost control of his emotions?

"Is that a threat, Allenon?" he asked with deceptive calm.

"Only the truth," the messenger deflected. "If the Haar isn't stopped, it will swallow your city, too. And there will be *nothing* left of the Bluescale court."

His eyes glanced over Kier and then me, and I had to force myself to stay calm. There was something dismissive in the look, and more I couldn't name. I wanted to show him exactly why he shouldn't underestimate me, but if I did that, everything I'd done so far would be for nothing. The goblin moon was two weeks away—all I had to do was hold on until then. I could get through one fucking meeting.

"I'm growing tired of these accusations," Kier said, eyes narrowed on the messenger. "You say you came to congratulate me and my wife, but here you are, slinging threats and slander."

Allenon's lip curled. The people on either side of him stood stiffly, like dressmakers' mannequins, emotionless and silent. Ugh, I looked exactly like them, sitting stiffly on my throne, not saying a damn word, pushing down my desire to kick Allenon in the balls.

"Your new wife," Allenon repeated, something I didn't like in his tone. His stare lingered on me; it took everything in me not to flash him a challenging grin and leap from my throne with a knife in my hand. "If you don't stop this ridiculous power play, your new wife will be little more than offal. I have no doubt you'll survive, and establish yourself as king of the wasteland, but you'll have no wife, and certainly no heir. The Haar will eat the flesh from her bones before your seed can even take."

I reared back, inhaling sharply. Okay, fuck this guy. That was the way he looked at me, what I'd been struggling to place—like I was a damn broodmare. Not even a pretty ornament to be admired the way I'd expected, but a fucking baby factory.

When Kier was dead, I was hunting down Allenon and putting a knife through his dick. I'd watch him bleed out slowly, excruciatingly over a period of days. The thought gave me a burst of calm, and I used it to stare at Alenon, unsettling and flat. I stared until he looked away, attention settling on Kier again as my husband leapt out of his throne.

But Allenon, clearly in love with the timbre of his own voice, was far from done. "And that's if the rebels don't mutilate her first. If she's dead, they'll get the war they want."

My heart thumped hard. His tone of voice screamed that he hoped that would happen. Would he try to kill me himself? Was he one of the bastards who'd blown up my wedding?

"If anyone lays a hand on my wife," Kier said, scarily calm again as he descended the dais, "they lose that hand."

Well. That shouldn't have been attractive.

Allenon didn't back down, pumped up on his own self-importance. To go toe-to-toe with a prince, he must have been pretty sure of his own social standing. Did he think he outranked Kier? *Did* he outrank him, as lover of the king? I wish I'd paid attention to hierarchies during my schooling, but I'd been too busy trying to avoid triggering my uncle's wrath and nursing my newest bruises to concentrate on much. I was far better at practical shit than book learning.

"You're very protective of someone you've known barely a fortnight," Allenon remarked, ignoring the look one of his buddies shot his way. Wow, so they *could* move. And *they* thought he was being a dick, too. "Not particularly smart, Kier, to show her as such an obvious weakness."

I was lucky everyone watched Kier as he stalked another step closer, radiating primal danger. No one saw my hands curl into fists in my lap, or the flash of teeth as my lip curled back.

So they'd use Kier's sweet, defenceless human wife against him? Make obvious threats so he did what they wanted? Great. Now everyone would come for me, and I'd have to kill them all.

But I had nothing better to do while I waited for the goblin moon. And it would keep me in shape... Okay, I was warming to the idea.

"Not particularly smart," Kier breathed, "to threaten my wife to my face, Allenon. If you think I wouldn't risk my father's wrath by killing you, think again. You make one move towards her, and you're dead."

Allenon's retinue swapped glances, all of them unsettled.

"Let me make this clear," Kier seethed, stalking another step closer. The others backed off, leaving Allenon standing alone. "I did not summon the Haar. I do not control it. And I am doing everything in my power to *stop* its destructive path. My sympathies to Skyan. Get the hell out of my castle."

Allenon's backup bowed swiftly and scurried down the long throne room to the door, slipping past the guards on either side of it and vanishing from sight. I smirked, just for one second before I smoothed the expression.

Allenon did the opposite to his retinue, taking a step closer, threat written in every line of his body. Fury and unease exploded through me. If he killed Kier, if he took my vengeance from me, stole Natasya's justice...

When Allenon took another step, I rose from my throne and descended the dais, drawing his attention. I moulded my face into an expression of nervous outrage, shrank my shoulders and twisted my hands in front of myself.

"You can threaten me," I said, in that soft, husky voice I'd practised earlier, "but I won't abide you hurting my husband."

Kier's gaze flickered with something I couldn't place when I laid a hand on his arm, angled close to him as if I was afraid of Allenon. I was annoyed to find my protectiveness was only ninety percent faked. That ten percent burned as I choked down the truth—if it came to it, I'd choose Kier over Allenon. I shouldn't be choosing *any* of these fuckers.

"How sweet," Allenon commented with a smile that made me want to kick out his front teeth. "She speaks, but only in defence of you. How well trained you have her, Kier."

Kier covered my hand on his arm and squeezed in warning. I pressed my lips together, swallowing the words I wanted to spit at the bastard messenger. *Think happy thoughts, think happy thoughts. Allenon's guts spilling out, his cut throat burbling with blood, the stupid choking sounds he'd make as he bled to death.*

"Get," Kier breathed, "out."

"You'll regret creating the Haar," Allenon sneered as he turned on his heel. "The king will make you pay for this attempted coup."

I watched him leave, Kier trembling with restraint at my

side. Was there some truth to Allenon's suspicion? Had Kier created it as an attempt to steal control of the Bluescale court? He held no affection for his brothers, that was for sure. If the same could be said of the king, would Kier do something this horrific just to oust them? Was that why he was so determined to stop the Haar? Was guilt driving him?

The door slammed behind Allenon, one guard following him at a nod from Kier, presumably making sure he left the castle.

"Well, that went well," I remarked, fairly optimistic all things considered. Allenon had thrown his weight around, but hadn't actually gained anything. And Kier and I had made a sound impression of a doting couple. Job done.

But Kier growled as he rounded on me, teeth bared and dark blue eyes wild. "*Well?* You think that went *well?*"

"No one died," I pointed out with a shrug.

His eyes flashed again, and a shudder rippled through me. I'd seen Kier pissed off but never like this. I wanted to back off a step, but held my ground, refusing to look weak.

"Leave us," Kier growled at the guards, and they peeled off the walls without a single word, some aiming for the big doors, others taking the small one we'd come through.

The second they were gone, Kier moved as fast as the wind, dragging me into him with a hand twisted in my loose hair.

"Allenon boasted about killing you to weaken me," Kier hissed, fingers tightening until I winced, surprising sparks shooting down my spine. "You're moving into my room. And I want you guarded at all times, not just with your maid. No more sneaking out of the castle, understood?"

"Or what?" I challenged, the loss of my freedom chafing. "You'll hurt me?"

Kier grabbed my hip with his free hand, slamming me

against his body as he hissed, "If I didn't know better, I'd think you liked being in danger."

"Hardly," I scoffed, ignoring the hot pulse of attraction. "If you think I'm sleeping in your bed, you're fucking delusional."

"Your name must be Delusional then," he returned smoothly, and so quickly that I blinked, impressed despite myself.

"In your damn dreams," I growled, my breathing laboured as his fingers twisted in my hair.

He kissed me before I could wrench back, his lips bruising and commanding. I gave in, kissing him for a second before I dragged myself away, hating the burnt sugar taste of him and craving more all at once.

"I'm not sleeping in your room," I insisted, putting distance between us and wincing at my throbbing scalp. "You're already sending guards with me when I leave the castle; I don't need one to follow me to the damn baths. And you owe me a sword," I added, heading for the little door.

"Zaba," Kier warned as I pulled the door open, his deep voice brushing me like a shiver.

I didn't respond.

"*Thanks a lot Allenon,*" I muttered under my breath, not turning back.

I was definitely cutting that fucker's dick off.

a week to go. The thought filled my mind as I slowly woke up, smothered by blankets with the covers pulled above my head. The thick scent of sandalwood and pine soap hit me a moment later, and I growled, my head suddenly full of my bastard husband.

"I told you to sleep on the sofa," I muttered, not opening my eyes.

He was supposed to sleep on the sofa in his living room, and I'd sleep in his bed to satisfy whatever possessive rage had gripped him since Allenon's visit. That was the rule. There was no exception to be made for sneaking into bed with me in the pale hours of morning.

"Kier," I hissed, slitting my eyes open—and finding him sound asleep.

I sighed, scratching the sleep from my eyes and watching him with a narrowed stare.

His facial hair was scruffier than it had been last week, lines cut into his deep gold face where they hadn't been. Allenon's visit had done a number on him, and not just because of the messenger's thinly veiled threats to me. The insinuation that Kier had summoned the Haar, plus the realisation that ninety percent of Bluscale lands were under fog and there was no way to stop it coming here ... it was taking a toll.

I ignored the pang in my chest. Honestly, killing him would be a mercy.

One week, and Natasya's death would be avenged. One week, and I'd finally be at peace.

I slipped out of the bed carefully, not wanting him to wake and distract me from my plan. He had a horrible habit of kissing the violence out of me, until I wanted to drown in him instead of actually *drowning* him. I couldn't afford to lose my head. I'd come here for a reason, and I'd be damned if three weeks of pretending to be a loyal wife would ruin it.

I grabbed a soft shirt and leggings from the drawer— Kier'd had all my things moved, without my say-so—and grabbed underwear, boots, and my sword—the holy trinity of necessary assassin equipment—before creeping out of the room to the bath.

Fancy ass prince Kier had his own private bath, which I made sure to help myself to as much as possible. There'd be no private baths when I killed him and fled the kingdom. Not until I sold my story and wrote my memoirs, anyway. Would they make a statue to commemorate my clever infiltration of the goblins? Maybe I'd have ropes of flowers draped across me like the war heroes of old on the anniversary of their great triumphs.

"Don't get ahead of yourself, Letta," I chided myself, putting my clothes in a bundle on the floor when I reached the bathroom, and running my fingers over the deep purple gemstone set in the wall.

A shiver raised the hairs on my arms whenever I used magic. I shouldn't have had even a drop; I was human. It still freaked me out, but as long as I thought of it as just another weapon, I could ignore the prickling unease. Besides, the bath bubbled with a layer of thick, rose-scented foam within seconds, curls of steam indicating the water was hot. I could easily get used to this.

I sank into the bath with a hiss, my eyes sliding shut when the hot water ate away all the tension that had bunched my muscles when I saw Kier sleeping beside me. It was a good thing, I told myself. He could let his guard down around me, which would make sneaking a knife to his throat in a week that much easier. But it left a rotting sensation in my stomach that he *trusted* me.

I ducked under the foam and water, scrubbing the sleep from my eyes, dragging my fingers through my hair. I could do this. It was what I'd worked for all these years, what had kept me going when I wanted to lay down and cry at the gaping hole in my chest. He'd stolen Natasya's life, butchered her. He deserved to die.

I eyed the sword I'd propped against a wooden cabinet full of liquid bubbles and hair potions. I should kill him with the sword he'd given me; that would be poetic justice. Besides, I hadn't had a choice to bloody my blade yet, and it was a shame to leave it unused. It was far too pretty to be merely decorative.

I floated in the water, letting my mind run through a dozen gruesome fantasies, ignoring the sharp pinch in my chest as I honed and refined each murderous plan until they were perfect. No matter what happened, I wouldn't be caught off guard.

Settled again, I climbed out, dried my body, and dressed. I could do this. Just another week, and it would all be over.

I hoped Kier would be gone from my room—technically his, but whatever—when I returned, but he was in the living room, throwing papers and vials out of a drawer as he searched for something.

I tucked away my irritation, and reminded myself I was a big, bad assassin and I could handle being in the same room as my husband.

"What have you lost?" I asked, propping a hip against the side of the sofa and blinking in surprise at the wild look Kier threw over his shoulder.

He was a sight to behold, his black hair dragged into the world's messiest bun and his eyes frantic, mouth pressed thin. "I had a healing stone here somewhere."

"Why do you need a healing stone?" I demanded, stalking across the room to him.

"It's not for me, don't worry," he replied, tipping out another drawer and rummaging through the spoils.

The relief that unwound through my chest was hideous.

"Then who?" I asked, eyeing the piles of junk on the rug. He'd better be planning to clean this up after he found the stone; *I* certainly wasn't doing it.

"The Haar has taken another village, but this time..."

"This time?" I prompted when he trailed off, kicking piles of letters aside. *Way to draw out the suspense, Kier.*

"It's different," he finished grimly. Mysteriously. Annoyingly.

"Thanks, that really paints a clear picture," I drawled.

He shot me a warning look, and I straightened, ignoring the things it did to me. *I'm going to kill him,* I wanted to scream at my body. *Stop wanting to fuck him, it's irritating!*

"The Haar is inside a woman," he snapped, his temper frayed as fuck. I blinked, watching as he hissed in satisfaction and lifted a deep jade stone from a pile of bottles and phials.

"Inside a woman?" I pressed, frowning. "You mean—it hasn't eaten her?"

"No," he confirmed tightly, stomping across the papers for the door without so much as a goodbye.

I followed, obviously.

"She's being brought to the castle infirmary," Kier explained, walking down the hallway outside so fast that I almost had to run to keep up. He took the stairs down to the ground floor two at a time, his black hair flying behind him like a banner.

I followed him in a dizzying path to a part of the castle Calanthe had only briefly shown me, the scent of lye and astringent medicine in the air.

"Stay outside," Kier barked, throwing open a white glossy door—and slamming it in my face.

I hissed at the indignity of it, grabbing the handle and swearing when the door didn't budge. Great. Fucking *magic*.

I paced away—and then swung back with a growl at Kier's rudeness, trying the door twice more before I gave up.

What did he mean the Haar was inside someone, instead of eating all the flesh and bloody bits from their bones? It had never done this before, that was for sure. But then, Kier said it had never laughed, and I knew what I'd heard in Cyana.

"Why do you even care?" I muttered at myself, but the answer was pretty fucking obvious. Being in Cyana surrounded by the Haar had left a mark on me.

I told myself I only waited in the hall so I could know what the fog was capable of, so I knew what to plan for, but that was a lie. I wanted to help.

I sneered at myself, sitting on the hard floor in a huff, resigned to waiting. Resigned to *caring*.

It was stupid; I'd only be in this place for another week,

and then I was going home. To the human lands, to Seagrave where I actually belonged. Where there was no Haar swallowing our towns and cities, devouring our people.

Not yet, anyway, a small voice added.

I tilted my head back against the wall, puffing out a breath. Could it crawl across the mountains and enter my home? It was fog; could *anything* keep it out?

Maybe I'd warn Celandrine, who could pass it on to our scientists. They must have been able to invent an acid or concoction that could neutralise the Haar before it ate us.

I glanced up at a rush of footsteps, but the two women in starched white dresses didn't do more than glance at me before rushing into the door where Kier had disappeared. I didn't bother testing the handle this time.

Why was I waiting? I should get up, go back to my room, and find something useful to do while Kier was busy. I'd managed to get him to drop the *guarded at all times* thing, but how long before he wavered on that agreement? I only had seven days left; I should be making the most of them. But I remained there on the floor, turning over a million things in my head.

"Brideling?" a voice asked, fuck knows how long later. I'd zoned out, staring at the white-painted bricks of the ceiling. "Hey, what are you doing out here?"

I blinked at Rook. "I honestly have no idea," I answered. "What are you doing here?"

I noted his long black coat, his thin braids pulled into a knot, and a bulging bag over his shoulder.

"Came to help," he said, and aimed for the door.

"Mm," I replied quietly, unable to figure out why my chest was so heavy. "Me, too."

Rook's bag rattled as he knocked on the door with his

knuckles, a nurse in bright white opening it within a second. "Come on, then," he said, startling the hell out of me when he angled his head, inviting me inside.

I didn't second guess myself, *or* Rook. I ignored my achy limbs and shot to my feet, ducking inside the door before it could lock me out again. I was the damn princess of this place; that was why it rankled. No one but me knew why I was really here. All they knew was I'd married their prince to buy a moment of peace, and I was trying my best to be a good princess. Shutting me out was a dick move, and it pissed me off.

Inside, the room was high-ceilinged and long enough to fit Kier's princely suite in it twice over. It was full of cubicles, beds, and curtained-off areas where people probably slept. The outside scents of soap and medicine were even sharper here, stinging my nose as I followed Rook and the nurse down the aisle towards where ten people gathered around a single bed by the window.

"What are you playing at?" Kier demanded when he spotted me—but he spoke to Rook, not me.

Rook drew his shoulders back, brown eyes narrowing. "I brought the potions you asked for," he bit out, carefully placing his bag on the vacant bed next door. "You're welcome."

"I don't want her in here," Kier growled, earning surprised looks from the medical staff.

I peered around Rook, my stomach dropping at the sight of a flame-haired woman with porcelain skin covered in a sheen of sweat. Her blankly staring eyes were ice-white. Haar-white.

Okay. I was starting to see what Kier meant by the fog being inside her.

"I'll just take her back outside, shall I?" Rook challenged, shocking the hell out of me by backing me up. "Let her sit on the floor for another three hours?"

Gods, had it been three hours? No wonder my ass hurt so badly. I shot Rook a quelling look; I could damn well defend myself.

"Besides, I need an assistant to hold my supplies while I administer them," Rook went on, his chin lifted and a warning on his dark face. It annoyed me that I liked him.

"Tell me what to do," I said to Rook, giving Kier a dirty look.

Just because I hadn't put out for him, he was being a dick to me in front of other people now? I thought that was something we only did in private.

As Rook instructed me to carefully set up the fat-bottomed potion bottles and narrow vials in a stand on a table between beds, Kier raked a gloved hand over his messy bun.

"We don't know the rules of the Haar anymore," he said quietly, his eyes burning the back of my neck since I refused to look at him. "I won't risk it getting you."

I pressed my mouth into a thin line, passing a lilac vial to Rook when he held out his hand for it. I wished Kier was lying, but I didn't sense artifice or deception. He was being a dick to protect me. Great. How was I supposed to feel about that?

Rook leaned over the red-haired woman to tip drops into her open eyes.

"Hmm," he said to himself, a scrunch between his dark brows. "Pass me the green one."

I dutifully un-stoppered a green bottle and put it in Rook's hand, holding my breath as he tipped the whole thing into the woman's mouth. Potioneer—that was what I'd heard people murmur about him over the weeks I'd been here.

"What's that *hmm* mean?" Kier demanded, holding the glowing green healing stone over the woman's throat.

"It's not a film over her eyes—it's embedded inside her. Like a parasite."

A shiver crawled down my spine. The green potion did nothing, and neither did the black vial I passed Rook next, or the opaque white syringe.

"You've tried fog's ruin, right?" I asked when a grey liquid that reflected green made the poor woman buck up and scream soundlessly, her mouth hanging open.

"It was the first thing we tried, ma'am," the nurse beside me answered with a scarily calm expression I envied. I'd never seen anything like this Haar infestation, and it made me cold all over.

"Kier, move your stone—" Rook's voice died in a twisted gasp when white smoke exploded from the woman's mouth.

One second, Kier was across from me, the next he was beside me, shoving me five steps away and surrounding me with a bubble of sapphire magic. Okay, he was definitely in hyper-protection mode. And he was right that I should have stayed outside. That fact burned.

The Haar rushed out of the woman's mouth, her eyes no longer flat white but glassy and sightless. Rook was the fastest to react, grabbing a familiar vial of fog's ruin and shattering it on the floor beneath the cloud of lightning-veined smoke.

It vanished instantly, but none of us moved for a good thirty seconds, watching the woman on the bed gasp a last breath before falling still, waiting to see if any more fog would explode from her.

When it didn't, I let out a slow breath, attempting to step

away from Kier. I was prevented by the arms banded around me like an iron cage. A low, furious growl raised the hairs on my arms.

"You can say it," Rook sighed, watching the woman. "Go on, say 'I told you so.'"

Kier's arms tightened around me, in danger of leaving bruises.

"Hold me any harder, and I'll cut you somewhere delicate," I said, so only Kier heard.

"Try it," he snarled in my ear.

"Is she dead?" one of the healers asked quietly, making Kier jump and release me a fraction.

"I'm afraid so," a male nurse replied, exchanging a tense glance with us all. "The Haar has left her, but she didn't survive."

"Shit," I breathed.

If the Haar got inside any of us, it was game over. None of my plans to kill Kier would matter, none of my hopes for the future would be realised.

"What can we do?" I asked the medical staff, looking at Rook and Kier, too. "What can we do to stop that happening to us, too?"

A grey-haired, ice-skinned man shook his head. He didn't need to speak, but his voice was like the final coffin nail, sealing our fate. "There's nothing that can be done."

27

*K*ier stormed off, brooding and silent, not long after the Haar-infested woman died, leaving the healers to deal with the woman's body. My mind full of arguments with myself, I helped Rook pack up his empty potion bottles and walked silently beside him down the pale grey hallways of the castle.

"Don't let Kier isolate himself," Rook said as we neared the main body of the castle. "He'll blame himself for this."

I made a sound in my throat. "How is this his fault? He can't control the Haar."

Rook slanted a look in my direction. "Well, you and I know that, but Kier's wired differently. He takes everything hard, especially after Danette."

"His sister?" I guessed, hating the tightness behind my ribs. What use was sympathy when I was going to kill him for murdering my own sister? Emotions were useless, senseless, and un-fucking-wanted. I should have been glad he knew what this pain felt like; he damn well deserved it.

Rook nodded, a thin braid falling from the knot on his head. "He blames himself for her death. Always has, and probably always will. His family don't make it easy on him, the bastards."

I could well believe that. If their messenger was as bad as Allenon, how much worse were the other royals? And couldn't I have been married to one of *them*? Couldn't one of the others have killed Natasya? I hated how tight my heart screwed up, how much I could understand Kier's pain, and I especially hated the magnetic pull towards him. Soul-mates, for fuck's sake.

I wished I didn't have to kill him. But justice had to be dealt.

"I hope I never meet them," I answered a beat too late, too deep in my thoughts.

"You and me both, brideling," Rook agreed. "Well, this is where we separate," he said when we reached the end of a hallway, my route carrying me towards the private royal rooms and his to the exit.

Rook hooked me into a squeezing hug before I could realise his intentions, his arm moving up and down my back in an infuriatingly comforting arc. "Try not to worry so much about this, okay? We've kept the Haar at bay from Lazankh so far, and we'll keep doing it."

He pulled back, his smile far softer than the usual flirty grin he gave me, and I felt like absolute shit for planning to take his best friend from him. Rook hadn't done anything wrong. Guilt gnawed holes in my stomach.

"See you around, brideling," he said, and ruffled my hair before stepping out of my personal space.

"Yeah," I agreed, choking down the swirling, oily feelings. "See you around, Rook."

Disquiet, I headed for the royal suite. Kier had an unopened bottle of something strong and foul in the court-yard, and I planned to drink an unhealthy amount of it. Was it a good idea to drown my fear and guilt with alcohol? No. Was that going to stop me? Also no.

"Kier?" I called, my feet dragging across the tiled floor when I reached the courtyard. The sky was turning royal blue through the dome overhead. I hadn't realised how late it was.

I dropped into a comfy chair with a groan, tilting my head back to soak up the air I badly needed after breathing hospital scent for hours. It weighed on me in a way I hadn't expected—the woman's death, the fight to save her, witnessing it all and being able to do fuck all to help.

When my dear husband didn't respond after a minute, I realised I was alone. Normally, I'd have loved the quiet, but right now the silence was full of the Haar's laugh and my sister's scream.

Gods, it was fucked up—wishing her killer was here so I didn't have to hear her imagined scream as he fucking *killed* her. Why couldn't her killer be one of his damned brothers? This was cruel.

I groaned, dropping my head and grabbing the bottle of amber liquid from the shelf under the table. It was full of crap—old newspapers, tobacco, letters he'd opened and discarded, doodles Xiona had done—mostly of dicks—and bottles of booze.

I didn't bother with a glass, cracking off the wax seal and applying directly to my mouth. It tasted like paint thinner, but the best stuff always did. I swallowed a few gulps and rested my head against the back of the chair, watching birds fly above the glass dome.

"What the hell am I gonna do?" I breathed, only safe to talk when I was alone.

I hated Kier with every fibre of my being, but ... I liked him. Hated him, and yet enjoyed the time we spent together.

The way his eyes flashed when I threatened to stab him fascinated me, and he'd somehow earned my admiration for his dedication to saving his people.

Why did he have to kill Natasya? The sick plot twist of this whole thing was, if he *hadn't* killed her, and if I'd still volunteered myself as his bride, I could have been happy.

I took another drink of paint thinner—sorry, expensive, delicious ambrosia—and groaned. Getting justice for Natasya would take something from me, would forever damage a part of me that I could never fix.

I drank a quarter of Kier's fancy booze and waited for him to come storming down the hall into the courtyard. But the sky grew darker overhead, and he never showed. With Rook's words loud in my ears, I cursed and shoved to my feet, ignoring my stomach's low growl as I set off through the castle to find my brooding husband.

What in hell was I thinking?

28

*I*t took me three hours to find him. I was forced to stop by the kitchens and charm a quiche from the cook to fill my stomach when I grew dizzy. I couldn't remember when I'd last eaten. I hadn't got breakfast before Kier rushed off to the hospital. Fuck—last night, then?

No wonder I'd devoured the whole thing and then shot pleading eyes at the deep blue woman, ignoring the horns curling over her blue rinse in favour of getting a strawberry bun.

I licked the last of the strawberry syrup off my fingers now as I climbed the delicate spiral staircase to the roof. It was the only place I hadn't checked, and unless Kier had wound up back at our rooms while I was searching, he had to be up here.

I pushed the door above my head, wincing at the obnoxious squeal of hinges, and dragged myself up on aching arms. I just wanted to *sleep*. But there was a knot in my chest that wound tighter with every passing hour, and it wasn't just Rook's plea urging me on now. It was my own damned worry.

Freezing air bit at my arms, face, and neck as I climbed onto the flat roof, casting an assessing stare over the blue stone chimneys, domes, and roofs all around us. The air smelled of bonfires, and orange light flickered from deeper in the city, mingling with the starlight from above.

I sighed heavily when I finally spotted Kier, slumped in an iron chair by a table at the edge of the roof. He barely moved as I crossed the roof, though he must have heard the gods-awful cry of the trap door opening.

"Still brooding, I see," I remarked, sliding onto the chair beside him and groaning at the relief of taking my weight off my feet. "You could make a professional sport of it. You'd get metals—a gold-medal winning brooder."

Kier slid a slow, dragging gaze in my direction. A pulse of warning went through my belly at the dull stare, devoid of any emotion but *seething* with darkness. Okay, so he was doing a little more than brooding.

You're here to kill him, I yelled at myself, even as I opened my hateful mouth and murmured, "It wasn't your fault. Don't be an idiot."

"Did I ask for your input?" Kier asked in a voice like danger.

I sat back in my chair, propping my aching feet on the base of the little iron table. "I'm your wife; I don't require your permission to hassle you."

"Leave me alone," he replied in an empty voice. "I don't want you here."

"You haven't wanted me from the start; why change now?" I pointed out wryly. "I'm not going anywhere, so deal with it."

The look he dragged my way was heavy with warning. I caged the part of me that kept hissing *he killed Natasya* and let out the pathetic part that reminded me we were married, and bound soul to soul for whatever good it would do. I held his glare with pure iron and stubbornness.

"Fine," he muttered, looking across the city, dismissing me.

I kicked off my shoes and settled in for the long haul. Hell, maybe I'd have a nap. The chair wasn't comfy, but I was drained and badly needed to be unconscious, so I doubted it would stop me.

I watched light flicker across the city, wondering if someone ought to do something about the fire before it razed a whole street to the ground. "We could plant silversweet at the borders of the city," I said after a few minutes of silence. "Spray all the houses with sugar syrup."

"The fields around Skyana are full of silversweet," Kier replied, voice as deep as an abyss. "It didn't save them."

"Your family probably got out," I said, watching him from the corner of my eye. "If Allenon did, they did too."

He nodded shallowly. "I know."

"So planting Silversweet is out," I sighed, thinking it through. "There must be something else we can do."

"The Haar's going to kill us all," he disagreed.

"I could really do without the defeatist attitude. What about shielding all of Lazankh?"

"It's already shielded," he replied flatly, a statue in the seat at my side.

"So shield it *more*," I pressed. "It can't hurt, right?"

"Leave it," he growled, but at least there was some emotion in his voice.

"If *you* give up, why should your people keep fighting? I thought you'd devoted yourself to serving them and keeping them safe? What use are you if you give up so easily?"

Kier laughed, twisted and bitter. "No use at all."

Ah, shit, this was harder than I thought. But I wasn't leaving him in this state.

"You've protected Lazankh," I reminded him, trying to find something positive. "All these people are alive. And Serul, don't forget about the good you've done there."

He turned to look at me, equal amounts of anger and suffering in his dark blue eyes. "Where do you think the woman who died today came from?"

I recoiled, my stomach twisting so suddenly that I felt sick. "No."

What about Ari and his mum...?

Kier growled a rough sigh and held out his arm. When I didn't immediately move, he huffed, "Get over here."

Sick and even sicker by what I was about to do, I pushed my aching body out of the iron chair and crawled into Kier's lap, comfort slamming into me when his arms came around me. The reassurance was torturous, and guilt choked me even as I relaxed into his body, resting my head on his shoulder.

Kier let out a shuddering sigh, and I felt a spark of something like magic flicker through my skin where his lips found my shoulder.

The knot in my chest finally unwound, letting more air to my lungs, and his embrace worked into my body until my muscles were loose and relaxed.

"Thank you," he said, so quietly I could have missed it. "For staying."

"No problem," I replied, far more casually than I felt.

Something had shifted between us, and I didn't know how to shift it back. I wasn't sure that was even possible.

I should have got up and gone back inside, but I stayed

there for a long time, letting Kier's illicit comfort wind through my bones after the day from hell.

The countdown to the goblin moon was starting to feel like a doomsday clock.

29

I hardly saw Kier all week, which suited me just fine. Being near him made my skin crawl and my heart race for reasons I didn't like to examine too closely. It was much better that he left me alone, only coming to the royal suite to crash on the sofa in the living room at dawn. Annoyingly, he'd had the doors to his balcony magically barred for safety reasons, so I couldn't test my escape plan while I waited for the goblin moon.

"Is it a metaphorical moon?" I asked myself, eyeing the flurry of goblins in both human and monstrous forms working on the big double doors to the courtyard. I slowed my approach, watching them. "Or an actual moon?"

Would it be blue? Or green, I supposed, since there were Greenheart goblins too. It didn't take a genius to figure out everything in their kingdom would be various shades of green, and their skin was probably emerald tones too.

I didn't know what to expect of the moon, other than it made the goblin royals weak and killable. Would it affect me, too? Did it mess with non-royal goblins? See, now would have been a good time to have had Calanthe on hand, but she wasn't working this evening.

"Your highness." A black-haired goblin bowed deeply upon noticing me, so tall he was still on my level even when ducking low. "The protections are almost finished. We should be done within the hour."

I nodded, like I actually cared whether Kier was protected or an assassin snuck in to murder him. I ignored the twinge in my chest at the thought of someone else killing him. He was *my* target, dammit.

"Thank you," I said, passing the man and quickly crossing the courtyard. It didn't feel right to have so many people in here—I'd grown used to it just being me and Kier, with the occasional drop-in from Xiona and Rook. I hadn't forgotten Odele's appearance, but the bustle filling the courtyard was so strange and unwanted that my hackles raised. I took the steps up to the second floor two at a time, but sat with my back to the wall, watching them, mistrustful.

True to the man's word, they finished covering the area in bright sapphire and purple magic an hour later, and packed up their things, slamming the doors behind themselves. I shuddered at the ripple of power that surged through the space when the door sealed. I knew enough about the protections to know those doors would stay locked until sunrise tomorrow, and not even an earthquake could open them.

"Fingers crossed the shields don't stop me going out the window," I breathed, hauling myself off the floor and stretching out my arms with a groan. If the doors were sealed, that meant Kier was already in here. Good.

I pulled air into my lungs and held it for four calming

seconds. I could do this. Everything came down to this, to tonight.

"I can do it, Natasya," I promised her.

I checked the dining hall, sitting rooms, and personal library, finally finding Kier in the living room he'd trashed a week ago.

He sat in the middle of a tornado of books and papers, his black hair in disarray and dark circles around his eyes.

I can do this.

I have to.

30

"What's all this?" I asked, stepping across a haphazard pile of yellowed papers. "You opening a library in our living room?"

Ugh, that word—our. I hated how easily it rolled off my tongue.

Kier grunted, not lifting his head from where it was bent over a heavy, leather-bound book. He'd been increasingly distracted all week, but this was next level.

"How long have you been here?" I asked, frowning at his creased black shirt and rumpled trousers.

"I'm trying to concentrate," he growled, flipping the page.

"Wow," I replied, drawing out the word. "He can *talk*. It's a goblin moon miracle."

Kier shot me a dirty look and went back to his book. "I'm trying to find a case of the Haar in our histories. Maybe it's happened before."

Good idea. Guilt twisted my gut at the realisation that his research would be unfinished. In a few short hours, as soon as the sun dropped and the moon rose, he'd be dead.

No. Someone would continue his cause, and fight back

the fog. Rook would, and Xiona. There'd be people left who cared, I promised myself to appease my guilt.

Probably because of that guilt—and because of the sick knot in my stomach at what I had to do later—I sat beside Kier on the rug and said, "Give me a book. I'll see what I can find, too."

The look of weary relief he shot me made me even sicker. I pushed away the feeling and got started on the book he dumped in front of me, glad for all the punishing reading lessons my uncle had me take.

"You want to know why I'm doing this," Kier said, hours later, when my back had grown stiff and my eyes ached from reading the tiny lines of text. I wanted to know how the hell I could read books in the goblin kingdoms, how we shared the same language, but now wasn't the time. "Why I was so affected by the woman's death."

I didn't look at him, didn't have the guts. "You don't have to tell me."

I didn't need him to start trusting me enough to confess his secrets. Not tonight.

"I swore when Danette died that I wouldn't lose anyone else," he confessed, his voice raw enough to shred my heart. "But I've failed spectacularly at that."

I didn't know what to say. I was such a damn coward.

"I didn't want you anywhere near that hospital," he went on, staring absently at the pile of read books in front of him. "I didn't want Rook there, either, but all the other potioneers are exiled, stuck halfway across the mountains, or dead."

My heart squeezed at the way his voice cracked. Now was not the time for sympathy, dammit! But fuck, his pain hurt—literally, crushing my chest. A bond thing, I presumed.

"So that's why you were so growly," I said, ignoring the strangled quality of my voice.

Kier nodded, glancing at me. Behind him, I realised the sky was dark through the windows, a blue sheen of magic coating the glass from edge to edge. "It was abhorrent to me, you being there. Especially when the Haar showed itself."

A growl entered his voice, twisting it. "All I could think about was losing you and Rook, too. I won't be responsible for anyone else's deaths."

Ugh, my sympathy was back, softening my heart so guilt could draw blood from its vulnerable flesh.

"I know what it's like to lose a sister," I said finally. "I haven't stopped thinking about her death, or her killer, since the moment I found her body."

Kier watched me, dark blue eyes gentle and considering. He didn't press for answers. I couldn't have got through that conversation anyway.

I pushed to my feet, flexing my fingers to work out the ache of holding heavy books for hours. "I should probably go to bed."

Should change my clothes and make sure I had everything packed in my bag, more like. I needed to be ready to go the second he was—

Fuck, I couldn't even think it. And now my throat was closing up, my stomach on the verge of purging everything I'd eaten today.

Kier watched me, sickening understanding on his tired face. "See you in the morning," he said, watching me.

I nodded and escaped into my room—his room.

"I can't do this," I choked out when I was alone, my back flat against the door and my hands shaking. I couldn't do it.

But talking about Natasya and the scars her murder had left on me had brought everything raging back to the surface. When I shut my eyes, I saw her discarded on the edge of Seagrave, cut in so many places that blood had soaked into the dirt, even her face bloody and mangled.

I dragged in a breath that cut me on the way down.

I couldn't do it—but I *had* to. He'd slaughtered my sister, had thrown her to the ground at the edge of the city as if she was trash. As if she meant nothing to anyone.

"Well, she means something to me," I hissed, hairs standing on end along my arms as deep blue light flickered in my ring. "And you don't get to take her from me without paying for it."

Equal parts sick and determined, I strode to the drawer where I'd stashed my bag full of plants, food, weapons, and supplies, and tried to pull some semblance of calm into my heart.

*I*t took Kier four hours to finally stop reading and pass out on the sofa; I kept my door cracked and listened to the steady rustle of pages turning and Kier's frustrated sighs until it was late. No one even attempted to breach the shields to kill him, though I kept an eye on the wall outside just in case some assassin tried to scale it.

The irony of being ready to kill an assassin to protect him ... and then to kill Kier myself wasn't lost on me. I told myself it was because he was my target, and mine to kill.

"You can do this," I breathed, readjusting the knife in my hand—the jewelled dagger Kier had given me in Cyana. The sword was too big for the intimate kill I planned.

I wanted him to know why I was killing him, but I knew if I tried to speak, I'd fuck this all up. So it would be quick. Merciful in a way he didn't deserve.

My heart could take nothing less.

I pushed back the nausea crawling up my throat as I edged the bedroom door open and crept down the hall. Shivers skated down my arms, raising goosebumps the closer I got to the living room. My heart punched my ribs so hard it must have left bruises.

I could do this. Natasya deserved justice. An eye for an eye.

My hand shook as I got close enough to see him, long black hair splayed on the cushion at the end of the sofa, his tall body scrunched up to fit but a foot hanging off the edge.

A physical pain splintered my heart like a lightning bolt, but I didn't let it stop me, ignoring the way my feet faltered on the soft rug between me and Kier. The fact that he didn't even murmur in his sleep meant he was either a deep sleeper or ... or he trusted me, and subconsciously registered me as safe.

I avoided looking at his face for as long as possible, barely breathing as I crept closer, all my years of sneaking around as an assassin, training for this moment, coming to fruition.

Here he was, vulnerable, killable. One glance out the window showed the moon full in the sky, a rich turquoise colour that was nowhere near natural. Nothing I'd ever seen in the human lands.

I could go home, I realised, my heart leaping. But it crashed when I looked at Kier, *really* looked at him. His face was slack with sleep, his chin resting on his hand and eyes shadowed with weeks' worth of stress. Maybe even months' worth; he'd been fighting for a ceasefire for fuck knows how long, culminating in marrying me.

I held my dagger tightly, nowhere near the easy grip I usually had, and ignored the near-crippling wrench in my chest that had a gasp choking off my air. I filled my mind with the sight of Natasya's brutalised body and brought my knife towards Kier's throat.

It'll be quick, I silently swore to him, hurting deep in my bones. *I promise.*

But my hand froze an inch above his vulnerable throat, and—I couldn't.

My face crumpled, my hand shaking harder. I couldn't do it, couldn't kill him. I had to, I fucking *had to*, or Natasya would never be avenged, but I *couldn't.*

I was going to throw up.

I lifted the knife an inch, but froze when Kier's eyes flew open, soft for a second when he spotted me. But then he realised I had a dagger to his throat. The dagger he'd gifted me, because I was a pathetic sap.

"Kier," I choked out when his fingers snapped around my wrist, dragging the blade away from his neck. "I couldn't—"

I couldn't get a breath, couldn't choke back the sickness, couldn't stand the deep, brutal pain in my chest as the mate bond revolted.

His deep laugh made me flinch, and I blinked awful, stabbing tears away as he rose, acute danger in the fluid movement.

"You've been waiting for the moon all this time," he snarled, his voice harsher than I'd ever heard it. "Waiting to kill me."

"But I couldn't," I protested, strangled and sharp. "Kier, I *couldn't—*"

He bared his teeth, needle-thin and numerous enough that cold pierced me. "You lied and pretended all this time, while you planned to kill me."

I had no defence. He was right. If I hadn't grown weak for him, he'd be dead right now.

"Is that why you married me? If Rook and Xiona hadn't been in the carriage, would you have tried to kill me minutes after we exchanged vows?" he demanded, wrenching me across the room by my wrist.

I struggled to keep up with his strides, choking down scraps of air.

He was supposed to be dead, and I was supposed to be going home. But I'd failed. I couldn't kill him, couldn't even fucking *hurt* him without pain crippling me.

"*Answer me!*" he roared, throwing me across the threshold to his bedroom.

"Yes," I rasped.

Kier shook his head, nothing but rage and hate and—fuck—*hurt* on his tanned face.

I lurched for the door the moment I realised what he meant to do, but Kier slammed it shut before I could get there. I hit the wood hard enough to bruise my temple and choked on a cry.

Tears finally splattered my cheeks. I hated every trail of salt that carved down my face, hated that I hurt as badly as when I'd first lost Natasya, hated that I wanted him to open the door so I could tell him *why* I hated him.

"*Kier!*" I screamed, my voice raw in a way I'd never heard it before.

"Please," I rasped, and slid down the door, folding up on the carpet and dragging my hands through my hair.

Everything I'd worked towards for years, and I'd ruined it. And I was *glad*. I was *glad* I hadn't avenged Natasya's death, hadn't taken revenge on Kier for what he'd done to her. I was fucking *relieved* I hadn't killed him, and I could not handle it a single bit.

A cry crushed my throat and tore its way free. I curled over my knees, and let the sobs obliterate me.

32

*I*t turned out that crying for hours while simultaneously trying to *stop* crying made you feel like shit the next day. I'd fallen asleep sitting against the door, and now I had one hell of a crick in my neck to go with the tight, stuffy feeling in my face and the rawness of my throat.

"Ugh," I groaned, hauling myself away from the bed and going for the balcony doors.

The protections would have worn off when the sun rose and Kier was safe from the goblin moon's vulnerability, but when I tugged on the handles, the door didn't budge.

"What the fuck?" I muttered, not in the mood for this. I wrenched hard on the handle but it stuck, so I went to the little window above Kier's desk. It didn't shift even a millimetre.

"You locked me in," I breathed, cold and furious all at once. "*You locked me in, you bastard?*" I yelled, loud and gritty.

He couldn't be killed now the sun had risen; what was the point in keeping me captive?

"To punish me," I realised with a rough laugh. "Of course."

I raised my voice and shouted, "I'll just wait here until you come to interrogate me, shall I? If I don't *starve to death* first!"

My stomach was already growling, and I needed to pee. This was going to be hell.

I stalked over to the bed and threw myself upon it, fuming even though Kier had been merciful. If someone had tried to kill me, I'd have slit their throat, no questions asked. I was lucky to be alive, but I couldn't think clearly enough to see that right now.

"When I get out of here, I'm going to..."

What? I'd been too weak to kill him, so what was I planning to do, exactly? Glare at him? If I was lucky, I'd be able to run past him and get the hell out of this place, but I knew that would never happen. I'd never been lucky once in my life; why start now?

I should have run the second I found out I couldn't kill him. I should never have stayed. If I'd done the smart thing, I could have been back in Seagrave by now.

But doing what? Enduring Celandrine's cutting guidance as she trained me to be a shining, useless figurehead to inspire our soldiers? Pass. Back to thieving and assassinating people, then. But being under the Scythe's thumb again made my skin crawl. I was my own master now, or I had been until Kier locked me in his room and sealed all the exits.

I didn't know what that made me now.

"A prisoner," I muttered, and glared at the balcony doors that refused to open for me.

A spark of inspiration had me hauling myself to my feet, reaching for the magic that lived inside me now and waiting for the ring to spark. The gemstone stayed shiny and ordinary and powerless. Great, now even the power I hadn't asked for had left me.

I fell back on the bed and waited for whatever was going to happen.

After a few hours—and being forced to piss in a vase—I realised nothing was going to happen at all.

They were leaving me here to rot.

33

*S*creams woke me near sunset, and I jerked awake, reaching under the pillow for my knife and exhaling in relief at the cold slide of it over my fingers. Kier had locked me in, but at least he'd locked me in with my hidden bag of supplies.

I'd managed to eat an apple and a chunk of bread, but I needed to ration what I had left in case I was locked in here for days. Or weeks.

Knife in hand, I got out of bed and pressed my ear to the door, but the screams were muffled here. I realised with a drop of icy dread that they came from outside the windows. In the city.

"Shit," I hissed, crossing the room. I already knew what I'd find when I stalked to the glass doors, and my stomach dropped to the floor at the confirmation.

The Haar blanketed the mountains and forest around Lazankh, silver veins of magic flashing through its opaque fog. I couldn't see the far edges of the city anymore, the towers and rooftops that had become unwittingly familiar to me these weeks swallowed from view.

Breath caught in my throat, and I backed up. Ran to the door and threw all my weight into pulling the handle. I slammed into the wood so hard pain exploded through my shoulder, and then did it again, starting to shake all over. The Haar was coming to devour the city and I was trapped in here with no way out.

"Let me out!" I screamed, slamming my fists into the wood, and gasping at the bright sapphire sparks that burst from my ring—and did absolutely nothing.

"Let me out, you bastard! I stopped before I could kill you; the least you can do is unlock the damn doors before I get eaten alive by fog!"

I knew I sounded hysterical, but with the Haar creeping across the city directly to the castle, *anyone* would lose their damn mind.

I hammered on the door until I bruised my fists, sparks of blue magic splashing the wood. I wanted my jaguar to burst to life, wanted it to eat through the door, wanted to get *out, out, out!*

My flight instincts had never thrummed so frantically before, my heart racing and hands shaking as I kept punching the door. If I couldn't break it with magic, maybe I could with brute strength.

I threw my bleeding fist into the door again—and the solid wood tore away. I tumbled forward with a cry, nearly shooting out of my skin with fear, but hands caught me. Gentle hands, not bruising hands.

"Rook...?"

The fury on his face told me we were no longer friends. Fair enough; I'd tried to murder his bestie.

He let go of me and braced his hands on the doorframe, stopping me before I could run. I could have stabbed him and pushed past, but I'd already tried to hurt

Kier, and the idea of wounding Rook made me genuinely nauseated.

"Why did you do it?" he demanded in a low growl, brown eyes narrowed on my face, reading everything I didn't bother to hide.

"He killed my sister," I replied, holding his glare. "He ripped her from me, and what he did to her..." I clenched my jaw, fighting back the tidal wave of grief.

"I've been waiting for a chance to kill him for years. And if I *had* been able to do it, he'd have deserved it. But I couldn't." I bared my teeth. "I *couldn't*, so get out of my damn way. I'm leaving."

I took a warning step, but didn't lift the dagger to threaten him. I didn't need to. Rook's eyes had widened, his face slack.

"Shit," he breathed, blinking at me. "*Shit*. Okay."

"*Move*, Rook," I growled, my back tingling as if I could already feel the Haar creeping closer.

"No," he blurted when I tried to duck under his arm. He caught me, pulling me into a hug and trapping my arms at my sides. "Listen to me, I get why you'd hate him. If he'd killed my sister, I'd make him pay, too. But *something* made you spare him."

"Stupidity," I sneered, my skin crawling at the thought of the fog encircling the castle, searching for me, laughing like it had in Ari's village.

Rook's gaze hardened as he peered down at me. "I think you care about him."

"If I did, that would make me a fucking idiot."

"He's out there in the middle of the fog," he told me, noting the tiny flinch I couldn't quite repress.

"He'll live," I dismissed his concern. "It parts for him, remember?"

"It used to," he agreed, sending a pulse of alarm through my chest. "Something changed."

His accusing eyes said *I'd* changed the fog, but he was delusional. I'd tried to slit Kier's throat, not fuck with the Haar. If I'd known how, I would have killed the fog weeks ago. I'd never get its laugh out of my head.

"Something changed," I echoed, my mind turning over the words. "It laughed at me in Cyana. Kier said it was impossible, but what if the Haar is mutating? What if it grows in power with every city it swallows?"

"Shit," Rook said, turning wan as he let go of me. "If destruction feeds it, the amount of power it has after devouring the capital alone..."

"Not good," I agreed. "Which is why I'll be leaving. Nice knowing you, Rook," I added and patted his shoulder as I edged past.

My supplies were in the bedroom, but escaping was suddenly more important than being prepared. If I could get out before the Haar caught up, I'd call that a win, and figure out what to eat and wear later.

"It's going to kill him," Rook said plainly. I ignored the sharp, prickly thing that lodged itself in my heart. "If you couldn't take his life, why are you okay with him dying now?"

"*What do you want me to do?*" I demanded, spinning to face him at the end of the hall. I didn't look at the sofa where I'd nearly killed my husband. "The Haar doesn't fear me like it does him; I'm *useless*."

"You can convince Kier to run and go into hiding like his family."

I snorted. "Sure, convince the most stubborn, protective man in the world to run away. Sounds realistic."

Rook blew out a hard breath, but didn't counter me. "Try. Please."

I shook my head, shoving aside visions of white fog surrounding Kier, its spears of silver magic striking him as the Haar devoured him.

"Tell him about your sister," Rook urged, holding out a pleading hand to me. I fixed my stare on his golden rings, avoiding his piercing stare. "Distract him, do whatever it takes to get him out of there. Please."

I was going to be sick if he kept begging me like that. "I nearly slit his throat last night, and you think I can save him today? You think he'd listen to a single thing I have to say?"

"Yes," Rook replied firmly. "You're his mate."

I groaned, dragging a hand through my ginger hair and yanking out knots. "I'm leaving. *You* go stop him."

Rook didn't stop me as I strode for the door, racing down the steps and into the courtyard where it was eerily silent. Beyond, in the castle proper, people ran in all directions, panic hanging as thick as the Haar. It hadn't reached us yet, but we all knew it was a matter of time.

"Will the prince's shields keep us safe?" a maid I vaguely recognised whispered to a gold-liveried man gripping her hand in white knuckles.

"Of course they will," he lied.

Most people I passed were in their goblin forms, as if blue skin and claws would save them from magical fog. Not that I could blame them; I had my knife in my hand for the same reason.

No one noticed the traitor princess in their midst. I made it to the door without being stopped, although I got a look that severely questioned my sanity from the butch woman guarding the door. Most people were barricading themselves in; I was on my way out.

"Oh," she said, straightening her back and offering a salute that made me feel worse than dirt. "Your highness. His highness is—"

"I know," I replied, flinching at the deadness in my voice. "I'm going to get him," I lied, hating the relief that crossed her face as I stalked out the castle and to gates on the verge of closing. People were sprinting through the streets to reach them, as if the castle would keep them safe.

"Don't you dare shut these gates until the Haar's close enough to kick you in the balls," I growled at the two guards holding the gates, one blue-black and the other as pale as ice. Both of them were tense with fear, but they startled at the sight of me.

I didn't know what made me say it, but I couldn't help the rage as I looked at the people running towards the gates; mothers clutching children, fathers shielding babies with their coats, teenagers helping grandparents along the slick cobbles of the streets.

"You save as many as you can," I ordered, and was glad I still had some authority left when they nodded and snapped to attention.

"Yes, ma'am."

Why did I bother? The shields wouldn't keep out the Haar; the castle wasn't safe. But the idea of the people streaming up the streets towards the beacon of safety Kier had made, only for the gates to swing shut in their faces ... I couldn't bear it.

"Run for the castle," I told everyone I passed, heading deeper into the city, running for the wall of opaque white fog sweeping like a wave over the blue rooftops.

It only struck me then, looking at magic flash like veins through the fog, that I hadn't lied to the woman guarding the castle's doors. I'd lied to *Rook*.

I was going to find Kier and drag him back even if it killed me.

34

*I*t turned out anger was as good an ammunition as fear for my magic as I raced into a solid wall of fog and rebounded off it *hard*. I landed on my ass with a cry that turned into a growl, eyes narrowed on the obstacle in front of me.

A laugh echoed through the clouds of opaque fog all around me, creeping closer. I *knew* the Haar had fucking laughed at me. Where was Kier so I could say *I told you so?*

"If you had a body, I'd make you bleed in so many places," I threatened the Haar, shoving myself back to my feet and ignoring the scrape on my leg that had left a nice hole on my leggings, baring my bloody thigh. I bet it made me look badass as I lifted my knife and blue magic spat from the jewels along the dagger's handle.

Fuck, I wanted my sword. Why had I left all my stuff in Kier's bedroom like an idiot?

The Haar's answering chuckle raised hairs on the back of my neck. I spun watching the smoky tendrils creep closer, like the limbs of a fucked up sea monster. Fear made me cold, but I refused to back down. It was too late to run now.

I honed my anger to a sharp edge, pushing back my dread, and slashed my dagger at the wall of magic-veined fog in front of me. I sensed the rest of the Haar closing in around me, sealing me in, so I stabbed harder, gritting my teeth when the blade glanced off like it was solid stone.

"Son of a bitch," I spat when the blade shattered on my next blow, the Haar's laughter rumbling down my back like a physical touch. I shuddered.

"Why are you doing this?" I demanded, moving the broken dagger into my other hand and slamming a fist into the wall instead. "What do you want?"

When my punch met the wall of fog, I swore it shivered, a ripple moving across the surface of it. I hit it again, and again, until my knuckles bled, and the fog under my hand softened, growing mouldable.

"What the hell *are* you?" I muttered. What kind of magic was this? Rook had said wild, raw magic when I first asked. But could raw magic laugh, change forms from smoke to solid, and be smart enough to block off the exits out of a city before sweeping in?

I flattened my hand to the wall and pushed, my brow knitting when it gave way a little, not solid at all. A cold rush went down my spine at the feeling of it between my fingers. Despite the magic flashing like lightning through it, I was never zapped, never hurt, which only made the whole thing stranger. Shouldn't I have started to feel weak by now? Shouldn't it be eating me?

"What are you?" I asked again, my teeth gritted against the bone-rattling terror that caught me in its grip. My anger had been swallowed entirely, until I was freezing and shaking.

"Za..." the Haar's faint, wispy voice echoed in my ears, and I flinched back.

I tried to pull my hand away, but the fog pressed its way between my fingers, solidified once more, and I realised ... a hand. It had become a *hand*, and a wrist, and its fingers were linked with mine, squeezing lightly.

I was only human; I screamed.

I wrenched my hand away with all my strength and stumbled away as fast as my jelly legs would carry me.

"Ba..." it rasped, and my heart stopped for a second.

Skittering away, I threw a panicked stare over my shoulder and whimpered at the sight of an arm pushing from the magic-veined wall of fog, followed by a shoulder, and then a torso—a whole fucking body.

My name—that's what it was trying to say. Zabaletta. *Za—ba—*

I turned and walked backwards, keeping eyes on the creature that crawled out of the wall as I fled. It was made of the same opaque white fog as the clouds of Haar, with magic flashing silver across its body and only faint hints at features on its face. Broad chested and tall, with bulges of fog for biceps and powerful thighs.

I waited for it to open its mouth and say *let*, forming the rest of my name. My retreat faltered when it started at the beginning again.

"Za—"

I realised I still held the broken dagger, and lifted it threateningly in front of me. Kier would have to fend for himself beyond that wall; I had to get out of here as fast as fucking possible.

"—Ba."

I shook my head, flinching as my own hair brushed the back of my neck. I should never have come to this place, never married Kier, never *stayed* as long as I had. I certainly shouldn't have raced across the city to save the husband who hated me—and who I myself hated with every bone in my body.

"Za—ba."

I froze between one step and the next, setting my foot down with a wobbly movement. Zaba. It wasn't calling me Zabaletta, but *Zaba*.

"Don't you fucking dare," I choked out, a tremble in my hand making the gems dance in my dagger. "Don't call me that."

Only one person called me that; only one ever had. Only Kier.

I clenched my jaw against a flood of emotion, my eyes stinging fiercely. "You don't get to fucking say that!" I shouted, my voice strangled.

The Haar shambled up the street in its new body, walking with jerky motions, like it hadn't figured out how to move yet. Emphasis on the yet—this thing was always growing, learning, and evolving. It wouldn't be long until there were a hundred Haar bodies, the fog's own damn army.

It wouldn't matter who won in the eternal human-goblin feud. We'd *all* be wiped out by the Haar's army. I knew devouring Bluescale lands was only the beginning; this thing was hungry, starving, and would swallow the world whole.

"Zaba," it said in its rough, whispery voice. My heart skipped. It got faster every time it spoke, grew more confident with every syllable.

I did not want to face the truth, but there it was shambling up the road towards me, calling my name—speaking the name *Kier* called me. Allenon had been right. Kier had created this thing somehow.

"Why?" I shouted, my heart slamming against my ribs, a

panicked bird trying to fly out of my doomed body. I couldn't blame it. "Why do all this, Kier? Why bother with the save-the-realm bullshit if you were the one destroying everything?"

I didn't understand how he'd fooled me. I'd believed him, believed how much he cared about his people. He'd stayed up until dawn searching for a solution, gods dammit; he'd been a complete wreck when that woman died. But *he'd* killed her.

I should have begged Allenon to take me with him when he left, should have scurried off to wherever the other royals had hidden. At least then I wouldn't have been sharing a castle with a mass fucking murderer. Ironic coming from an assassin, but the Haar—and now Kier—scared the shit out of me.

"*Why?*" I screamed, loud enough that the Haar's jerking steps faltered and its vaguely face-shaped thing pointed at me.

"Zaba."

"Yes, we've established you know my name," I growled, anger biting through my fear for the moment. I clenched my fist around the dagger, light flashing through the stones embedded in it. "I want to know why you've killed all these people. Time's ticking, Kier. Answer me."

The Haar tilted its head, the various clouds writhing along the street pausing. The effect was eerie as hell, and I backed up a step, checking it wasn't about to grab me from behind.

"Kier," the Haar said, head still tilted at an unnatural angle, watching me.

"Yeah, that's *you*, asshole. Or at least your master."

"Kier," it repeated in a raspy murmur, and I flinched back

several steps as the solid wall of fog and magic collapsed in a rush, pooling like an ocean at the bottom of the street.

Kier—actual Kier, with his long black hair, deeply tanned skin, and pure black wardrobe—lay on the cobbles, not drained to death but certainly unconscious.

"Okay," I breathed to myself. "So it might *not* be Kier, after all. Unless it's turned on him."

And if it had, that didn't bode well for me.

"What do you want?" I asked, changing tack. It wanted something—everything in the damn world wanted something. Magic flared from my ring and my dagger in response to the threat to my life; I kept the gem-encrusted handle between me and the Haar as if it would save me.

"Want," it echoed, looking between me and Kier's prone form. "Want."

Could it speak for itself? It was just repeating what I said, like a creepy echo.

"Fame? Money? Power? Status? Complete domination of the known world?" I reeled off. It had to be one of them, for fuck's sake. And why was I interviewing a damn fog monster anyway?

I knew why—my eyes gave it away by drifting to Kier's unconscious body—but I didn't want to admit it to myself. I couldn't leave him, even if he had done this whole thing.

If he had, I wanted to know why—*needed* to. If he hadn't, he didn't deserve this shit.

He killed Natasya, I reminded myself, touching the necklace around my throat. I should walk away, leave him here with wither and rot. He deserved it.

I think you care about him, Rook had said. Observant bastard.

"Cuh..." the Haar said, taking a wobbly step towards me that I met with three backwards steps.

"Cuh *what*? I can think of a word to describe you that sounds something similar," I spat shakily, distantly aware I was having a conversation with *fog* and *magic*.

I wanted to go back to Celandrine's boring figurehead training. At least there were no talking fog monsters in her pretty halls and intimidating barracks.

"Com ... plete," the Haar said in a slur.

"Huh?" I waved my broken dagger at it. "Complete? You want complete? Want to *be* complete? What in hell does that mean, you homicidal maniac?"

I needed to find a way around the creature and to Kier, and the most obvious way was across the rooftops. But would the Haar follow me? It was fog; it'd probably just float after me.

The Haar lifted a hand in silent plea. "Want complete."

"Alright, how about you release Kier, and I'll get you the *complete* you want so badly?" Under my breath I added, "Whatever the hell that even means."

The Haar moved closer to me instead of doing what I told it to, and I growled a breath. Right, we were doing this the hard way.

"Stay," I said sternly, like I was talking to a dog.

"Stay," it echoed.

I didn't know if it even knew the meaning of words, but I didn't hang around to ask.

I grabbed the pipe running up the side of the building to my left and scaled it as fast as I could without my gloves or rubber shoes. My knees were still a little jellified, which wasn't great for climbing, but I gritted my teeth and kept hauling myself up until I reached the roof.

A quick glance down showed the Haar's body looking at me, his head tilted back. Tendrils of smoky clouds were already following me, so I dragged a short breath into my lungs and cursed my damned feelings as I ran across the rooftop and leapt to the next one.

Only muscle memory allowed me to catch the guttering and drag myself to safety. I kept moving, running on to the next roof and the next, until Kier lay on the cobbles below me, a ring of magic-laced fog around him.

"Okay, *fuck*, it's *fine*," I said in a rush, my attempt to reassure myself pathetic. "How many times have you done something like this?" I asked myself. I might as well—talking to fog was surely a sign of insanity, so why not add talking to myself to the list of warning signs?

"How many buildings have you broken into, and lived? How many times have you climbed down from a similar height? You got this."

I didn't, but at least my pep talk strengthened my determination.

"You better give me the answers I want after this," I growled at my unconscious husband and began the descent.

I hung from the edge of the building for a prolonged, blood-chilling second, getting my bearings.

"Stay!" the Haar shouted, panic in its wispy voice. "Zaba, *stay!*"

"Not fucking likely," I bit out, and adjusted the placement of my legs before I dropped, grabbing the windowsill below by instinct alone. Breath rushed from my lungs, but I was steadier now; I had a clear path of descent.

As long as I didn't let go, that was. Then, I'd be splattered on the stone below.

"Stay," the Haar shouted, its voice getting louder, stronger. Not quite like Kier's, but close enough that it gave me goosebumps. "*Zaba, stay.*"

"Mind your own business," I bit out, climbing down to

the next windowsill via a sturdy pipe, and then dropping cat-like to the ground.

"Hey, asshole," I greeted Kier's slack face "Miss me?"

35

I toed Kier's body with my boot before kneeling and checking for a pulse. My relief was a hideous thing; I blocked it out as I rolled Kier onto his back and made sure he was breathing, too.

"Wake up, you bastard," I growled in his face, shoving his shoulder.

"Wake up," the raspy voice of the Haar repeated just behind me.

Chills crawled across my body as Kier shot upright, grabbing my shoulders.

His fingers dug into my skin, his eyes frantic but blue—not white from edge to edge. The Haar hadn't possessed him like it did the woman who died.

"You have some explaining to do," I said coldly, prying his fingers from my shoulders and ignoring the way they shook and clung to me, as if he didn't want to lose the contact.

I shifted so I could keep the Haar *and* Kier in my sight, the creature hovering at the edge of a ring of indistinct fog around me and Kier. Not attempting to grab and devour us—yet.

"Call off your monster," I spat. "And tell me why the hell you've created it."

I expected bullshit and bravado, but Kier hung his head, dark hair obscuring his face. "I didn't know."

"Stay," the Haar said, lifting its hand at me, like it was asking. I glanced sharply away, keeping it in the corner of my eye but not looking at it full-on. I didn't want to know why the Haar was asking me to stay.

"Call it off," I repeated, ignoring the lump in my throat.

"I can't," Kier rasped, lifting his head to look at me, such a depth of misery in his eyes that it physically hurt to see. But I refused to show any sympathy.

"Tell it to *back off*, Kier. You and I need to have a conversation."

Kier's gaze cleared, and he seemed to remember who I was—not his doting wife, but the woman who'd tried to kill him.

"Before you start," I growled, turning to watch the Haar as it circled us, its solid white body flashing with veins of magic, "I just walked through this damn fog to save your life. So let's table your anger at my failed assassination attempt."

I pushed to my feet now he wasn't on death's door, splitting my attention between the Haar, the eddies of fog swirling in a ring around us, and Kier as he rose, watching me suspiciously.

"Have you even *tried* to command it?" I demanded sourly, ignoring the whispery hiss the Haar made.

"It's fixated on *you*," Kier fired back, batting hair out of his face as he glared at the Haar. "How do I know *you* haven't taken control of it?"

With a rush of unease, I noticed the Haar's attention did follow me whenever he moved.

"You're deflecting," I accused. "Just tell it to disperse and leave the city."

"You tell it—" Kier growled, taking a step towards me, tension and threat lining his body.

The Haar let out a piercing cry and leapt between me and my husband, it's back to me as it growled in Kier's face.

"Okay," I admitted, backing up. "This does look sketchy."

"Leave the city," the Haar growled at Kier, echoing my words from a second ago. Cold spread throughout me, and I locked eyes with Kier over its shoulder as I backed away. We might have been enemies, but right now we had to put that aside and find a way out of this.

I forgot about the ring of twisting Haar until I stepped into it, and the fog creature shuddered. Cold spiralled around my ankle, and I kicked sharply at the tendril that wound around me. It should have been as bodiless as mist, but somehow it held onto me and didn't let go. It trapped my foot in place so more of its fog could wrap around my legs.

"Kier," I choked out. "Find a way to end this. Or I'm coming back from the dead to haunt your ass."

Something flickered in his eyes when we made eye contact. He nodded, jaw clenching.

"Enough," he ordered the Haar, making my stomach flip when he reached out and grabbed the creature's shoulder— solid enough to make contact. "I might have given you life, but I never told you to do this. *Enough*."

The Haar cocked a head, and a very bad feeling swirled through me. I fought the fog wrapped around me like octopus tentacles, trying to kick with what little movement I could make, clawing at the fog. All I did was gouge my own skin; despite how strong the Haar was, it flowed around me like air.

"A little *faster*, husband," I bit out, my breathing short as the tendrils wound up my chest. If it reached my throat, would it cut off my air? It crawled down my arms, knocking the pathetic knife from my hand. I had no way to defend myself.

"*No*," the Haar growled in Kier's face, rearing back its hand and—and punching Kier hard enough to break his nose.

Okay, so the Haar knew how to brawl. That was ... I had no idea what it was, actually.

"Leave him alone, you misty psychopath!" I spat, hissing mad.

The Haar froze and turned, watching the way I fought against its hold. "Stay, Zaba," it said, voice softening.

"Go to hell," I snapped, baring my teeth.

My breath stuttered when Kier charged at the Haar from behind, using its focus on me against it as he leapt on the creature's back like a maniac. I saw why he'd done it a moment later; Rook, Xiona, and a handful of guards were sprinting down the street towards us, magic flashing around them.

"Why aren't you using magic?" I spat at Kier. That would have been really fucking handy right now. I looked pointedly at the ring on my finger, but all it did was throw out pathetic sparks.

"I can't," Kier said through clenched teeth, holding on as the Haar spun, a wretched hissing sound in its throat as it tried to throw off Kier. "Tried."

I fought the fog binding me harder, urging my rage to transmute into magic and explode through my ring. But if Kier couldn't use his immense power, I couldn't get more than pathetic little flashes, and the tendrils swallowed those like they were honey.

Honey ... if we'd had fog's ruin, something sweet to appease the creature, we could get out of this. If only I hadn't left my bag in Kier's room when I fled; I could have used the silversweet to bribe it.

But why did sugar syrup and a sweet plant calm the Haar from its murderous path, anyway? There was too much I didn't understand here, and putting it together was making my head hurt. I scrambled for facts.

- Sweetness calmed it.
- Kier's presence scattered it—or had, at least.
- My attempt to kill Kier had altered that, if Rook was to be believed.
- It had sprung into existence the same week Kier's sister died.
- It devoured everything in its path, with an endless hunger.
- It now looked and sounded too close to Kier to be dismissed as anything but his creation.

So did any of that tell me? Other than Kier was too powerful and dangerously insane, and needed to get help for his grief—

His grief...

"Kier," I breathed, watching him grapple with the fog creature, silver lightning flashing across its body and zapping Kier. He endured it in silence, teeth gritted, eyes narrowed. Like he was used to handling pain. It occurred to me that I didn't know why he lived apart from his family in the capital, didn't know anything about his past actually.

"Did you ever find anything in your research about

immense emotions turning to magic?" I asked, flexing my fingers and testing the ironclad grip of the Haar around my wrist. I needed to get out of this ring of fog, and fast.

"No," he bit out—and then paused, long enough for the Haar to buck and throw him off.

"*Stop it!*" I screamed when Kier hit the ground hard enough that I expected to see broken bones poking out of his skin. He was very, very lucky that they weren't. "Hey, Haar fucker, *look at me.*"

Kier had thought of something—I saw it, even as he hissed in pain and pulled his arm close to his body, cradling it in a way that I guessed his shoulder had dislocated.

The Haar faced me, taking a step nearer. I locked down the shot of instinctual, crippling fear. I needed to think, to be clear.

"You wanted me to stay, right?" I bargained with it, eyes locked on the vague shape of a face—the slight slope of a nose, the shallow dips of eyes, the curve of a mouth. "Stop hurting Kier, and I'll think about it."

I wouldn't promise it a damn thing, but I could lead it on if it kept my husband alive. Ugh, Rook was right. I had feelings for him.

Disgusting.

"Stop hurting Kier," the Haar parrotted. It took all my willpower to keep my attention on the creature even as shadows moved behind it—the cavalry coming to our aid.

"Exactly. Don't hurt him, focus on me."

Breathless hope that I might get out of this alive made me shivery and weak, but I had to hold on. Pride came before a fall and all that. If I let my guard down, that was an easy way to get murdered. Or judging by the way this Haar looked at me, it was a good way to get abducted and kept as a fog monster's little wifey.

It was Kier, at least in part—did it see me as its wife? Its mate? Was that why it was so obsessed with me? I shuddered, cold streaking through me.

"The Fury," Kier said, watching me intently. "About a hundred years ago, the Bluescale king—my great grandfather—created a monster. We call it the Fury. His rage at his daughters became so great that it took on a life of its own."

My head spun, even as my heart ached.

"Oh, Kier," I sighed—and straightened at the Haar's hiss. *Right*, it wanted to be the centre of my attention. Got it.

So I spoke to the creature instead, my heart hammering as it leaned closer at the sound of my voice, a low hum in its throat like a purr.

"I think you're Kier's grief come to life," I breathed, swallowing hard. "I think he lost his sister, and couldn't handle the pain, and that's why you were created the same week."

Kier inhaled sharply, retreating a step and shaking his head. "I didn't. I never meant to—"

"Watch it!" Xiona shouted as Kier veered dangerously close to the ring of fog. Not a good sign for me—they wouldn't be so worried if they had a way of freeing me, right?

"Stay calm, brideling," Rook murmured, probably seeing my panic. "You're gonna be fine."

"She tried to fucking *kill* him," Xiona spat. "Let the bitch rot."

One second the Haar was in front of me, the next it was outside the circle with its white hand around Xiona's golden throat, sparks of silver zapping her skin.

Her scream was horrific, so powerful it made the tendrils of fog holding me waver. I wrenched as hard as I could, teeth gritted on a scream as my ankle threatened to tear out of its socket to match Kier's fucked up shoulder.

Sapphire light flickered in my ring, and I clenched my jaw, willing it to form a shield around me, to keep me safe the way Kier's magic protected the castle on the hill.

A watery light rippled up my hand, barely more than a sheen across my palm, but it dissolved the fog around my arms, and I thrust it at my legs, burning away the Haar's mark there, too.

I couldn't breathe, struggling to hold onto the tiny shield. But in a dizzying second, I was free.

Rook was there to catch me when I scrambled away, his hands gentle but tight enough to tell me how afraid he was. "I've got you, brideling. You're alright, now."

"Other than having a murderous fog monster trying to kill me, you mean?"

"Other than that, yeah," he agreed with a strained laugh.

"Fog's ruin?" I asked, my heart beating so fast I could feel it all over my body.

Rook placed a vial in my hand. "That's why it took us so long to get here; the store was plundered."

"No surprise," I drawled. I would have done the same thing if I'd thought of it.

I backed up a step as the fog circle flared higher, and the Haar's face aimed my way, betrayal in its rough voice as it said, "Zaba. Stay."

"Sorry, buddy. You might have been made by my husband, but that doesn't make me your plaything."

"Zaba," it replied, aching and melancholy. My heart squeezed pathetically. Great, now I was feeling sympathy for a lump of fog.

"Leave her," Xiona spat, and I shot an edgy look across the circle as Kier marched around it. In my direction.

"I take it you haven't told him," Rook drawled quietly,

pulling a bottle of something glowing and green from his bag and shattering it inside the fog circle.

The Haar screamed, and I flinched. I swore I felt an ache in my chest, and a sickening thought occurred to me: was the Haar a thing of Kier's creation ... or was it a *part* of him? The part that had broken when Danette wasted away?

"You tried to kill me," Kier growled, stalking around the ring, his shoulders tight under his tattered black skirt and his hands curled into fists.

"Yeah," I agreed with a tight shrug. I was ready to kick him in the balls if necessary.

"You came here to save me," he went on, snarling and so deep it reverberated in my ribs the closer he got, Xiona stalking after him.

"Yeah..." I agreed, my voice weaker. He was pissed I'd tried to help him?

My whole body jolted when he grabbed me and dragged me against his body, hugging me so tight I swore my bones rearranged.

Holy fucking gods, I needed this.

I melted against Kier with a ragged breath, my head thudding against his chest. I was too jittery and scared to hate him right now; all I could do was grab whatever comfort I could.

"I don't underst—" Kier began, but the Haar let out a soul-piercing scream and we flinched apart to cover our ears.

The creature's attention was on me—and Kier. As if our touch had harmed it.

What the hell...?

I pressed my hands harder over my ears, my head pounding as it kept screaming, and the distinct edges of its body blurred, sifting into fog again. I opened my mouth, but

I didn't know what I planned to say. The Haar burst into a cloud of fog before I could get out even a word, and I recoiled, expecting it to rush at me.

Instead, it spread into the city, leaving an empty ring around us.

"We can't let it reach the castle," I shouted, lowering my hands slightly and relieved that the scream had dissolved. "It's full of people."

"Like you give a shit," Xiona spat, fire in her striking amber eyes. "Go rot in hell, traitor."

There was so much acid in that last word that I realised she'd begun to trust me, too, and felt as betrayed as Rook did by me trying to kill their friend.

"Believe what you want, but what's left of your people are up there, thinking they're safe in the castle. You might want to save them."

I started up the hill without them, my emotions too wrung out to say much more. There was a deep pain behind my ribs, and a thread I swore tugged me to the castle—to the Haar.

Ugh, this was a mess. Did Kier even realise the kind of power his creature had? It was its own person now, learning and mutating every minute.

"Maybe you and Zabaletta should talk," Rook suggested quietly to Kier, following after me with Xiona reluctantly in tow, weapons clattering on her body. I would have killed for a knife, but something told me she wouldn't be up for lending me one of hers.

My shattered dagger was somewhere back there, swallowed by the fog, its power gone. All I had was my ring—but that hadn't been enough back in Cyana, I reminded myself.

"When the Haar's gone," Kier said to Rook, as if we couldn't all hear their conversation.

The Haar's scream rattled around my head, stabbing my ears, even though it had surged to the castle. Where it could do worse damage. In revenge, because it was jealous of Kier?

"We should just kill her and be done with it," Xiona muttered—and shut up when Kier snarled.

A shiver skated down my spine as I trudged up the road and through the city. At least Kier seemed to be back on Team Letta, and he hadn't shot down the idea of a conversation. Risking my life to save his had worked wonders. I still felt like a fucking idiot, though. Developing feelings was never part of the plan.

"Oh shit," I breathed, stopping dead as we rounded a corner with a clear view of the castle's towers and spires.

A plume of fog hulked on top of it, kept at bay by Kier's shield—for now. How long until it ate through the magic like it devoured everything else? How long until it murdered all the people sheltering inside?

36

"*P*lan, Kier?" Rook asked tightly, coming to stand beside me to stare at the dome of lightning-wreathed fog.

Kier shook his head. He didn't have one.

"I've got an idea," Xiona said, shooting me a dirty look, like I shouldn't be hearing this. "You asked me to look into those emerald cannons, Kier."

"You have some?" Kier asked, taking a step towards her, his eyes intent.

"Better." Xiona's cruel grin was a thing of beauty. I was actually nervous to be on her bad side, even knowing I could handle myself. "I had my team find a way to shoot fog's ruin instead of gem dust."

A laugh of disbelief shot from me. "That's fucking genius."

Xiona only levelled a scathing look on me, her beautiful face cold. "You're not having one. If you want to be helpful, go feed yourself to the Haar."

With that lovely comment, she stalked across the street and vanished down a side street.

"Should we be worried about her?" Rook asked, watching the place she'd vanished.

"We should be worried about the rest of us with her in that mood," Kier drawled, but he watched the street until she returned a few minutes later, arms full of something I'd never seen before. It looked like a mini cannon, but with a giant hunk of hollowed-out crystal where the chamber would be.

"Here," she growled, thrusting one at Kier and another at Rook. "You—" she said, spinning to me with a snarl.

"Yeah, yeah," I interrupted, rolling my eyes even as I fixed my attention on the Haar crouched above the castle. There were fractures in the sheer blue surface, deep and widespread. Could Kier feel those cracks spreading? Did they hurt him? "You want me to die a horrible, gory death. Got it, Xiona."

"Don't say my name," she hissed fiercely.

"This isn't helping," Kier bit out, lifting his cannon and storming in the direction of the castle. My stomach flipped both at the idea of him being back near the Haar and *me* going near the fog without one of those fancy weapons. "Xio, tell me how to work this."

"Empower it like any sword," she said, as if he was stupid.

Chills gripped me as I followed him, more cracks spreading across the shield wrapped around the castle. I choked on a vulgar word when it shattered with a loud groan, and Kier dropped to one knee on the ground.

I caught his arm before he could hit the stones face-first, gritting my teeth at the effort of holding him up until Rook grabbed his other arm. Xiona scooped up the weapon as it slid from Kier's hand.

"Stop the Haar," Kier said through gritted teeth, his pain so sharp that it carved a hole through my chest. I squeezed his arm and refused to let go. I wasn't sure I physically *could* peel my fingers off him; I only held him tighter. "Don't let it—"

He bucked with pain as shards of cobalt magic fell from the castle, like broken glass clattering to the ground before winking out.

I shot a panicked look at Rook, who shrugged but rifled through his bag for a tiny jar of something yellow and fragrant. Kier didn't complain as his friend smeared the foul stuff on his throat, trusting him completely.

A shadow moved over us, and I tensed, ready to leap into battle to defend my mate with my bare hands if necessary, but it was only Xiona stalking past, her white hair like a bright star as she lifted both guns. Bright magic flashed through both, and it hit me how much power she had—not as much as the royals, but a seriously intimidating amount —as a stream of searing hot magic shot from each barrel.

"Mother's breath, Xio," Rook hissed. "Be careful."

"I'll be careful when that fog bastard stops killing my people!" she yelled back.

I was with Xiona on this. There was a time for caution, and now was not it.

"Come on," I said, squeezing Kier's arm and not allowing myself to linger on the warmth of his muscle under my hand. "Up you get."

"Can't," he bit out, even as he pushed off the cobbles, Rook supporting him with a grunt at his weight.

"Can," I pointed out dryly, my heart skipping at the look he shot my way—wry and amused.

It hit me that there was nothing stopping me having a real relationship with Kier, only my own stubbornness. Natasya could hate me for it, but she'd been gone for so long that I wasn't even sure what she'd say about this whole mess.

Natasya had been the noble one, the protector, but she'd fought for us to be happy, to be free to make our own choices, no matter how disastrous they were.

If we got rid of the Haar, or found a way for Kier to control it, I could have a life here. All I had to do was stop hating Kier, stop sneering at goblins like they were my enemy, and admit that maybe we weren't so different. Kier was broken by losing his sister; I was, too.

"Why did Rook say we need to talk?" Kier asked, giving me a long look and no doubt noticing the way I tensed.

I honestly had no idea how that conversation was going to go.

Hey, sorry I married you to kill you in revenge for you killing my sister, but I want to be your wife for real now.

Nope.

I shrugged, guiding Kier after Xiona. Nice of her to leave us with one magically-powered weapon and hog two for herself. Real nice. "No idea."

Rook threw a betrayed glare my way; I pretended not to notice.

"Less talking, more Haar destroying," I added, wincing at the silver-veined fog creeping down the castle from the spires and towers. Bricks had begun crumbling, pock-marked and weak. How long before the structure broke down?

"Oh," I added, "And I think the Haar might be a part of you, so try not to actually *kill* it, yeah? It could kill you, too."

"What?" he demanded, sounding better, stronger. Whatever the yellow paste was, it seemed to be working. Thank gods for Rook's potions bag.

"Shit!" I shouted, throwing my body into Kier to knock him aside when a giant chunk of masonry came plummeting towards us. I yelped when it flattened a section of the castle wall, spraying debris and dust everywhere.

Grit covered my face even as I ducked close to Kier, the two of us falling into the wall of a nearby house and Rook... where was Rook?

"*Rook?*" I shouted, frantically scanning the dust-covered street. Where the hell was he, and why was I panicking so much at the thought of him being crushed to death somewhere?

"Here," he called from across the street, and I exhaled hard at the sight of him cowering in a doorway, his arms over his head.

A soul-wrenching scream came from within the wall, and I jerked forward, a buzz of alarm raising all the hairs down my arms.

"Xio," Kier choked out, grabbing my hand and tugging me away from the building towards the gaping maw in the wall.

"What's the plan?" Rook asked, running after us breathlessly.

I waited for Kier to speak, and my stomach dropped when he only urged us onto castle grounds, racing towards that scream.

"Great, we're gonna die," I groaned. "This is *not* how I wanted to die."

I'd wanted to die bathed in the blood of my worst enemy, but that was no longer as appealing, given I had awful, genuine feelings for him.

"Watch out!" Rook shouted, and the three of us flattened ourselves to the cold grey brick of the castle when a giant shard of the lapis spire fell like a shooting star, exploding when it hit the ground.

Kier spun me, pressing my face into his chest and

shielding my head. His body rumbled with a growl, and I shuddered as it moved through me, blocking out the sound of shattering bricks and groaning stone for a second.

"It's getting closer!" Rook shouted over the creaking and smashing. "The Haar's coming down!"

It slithered down the castle like a poisonous fog, leaving ruination wherever it trailed. I tipped my head back to watch as it glided down, the castle peeking out through its silver-veined tendrils. Could I still talk to it like I'd spoken to the fog creature? Was it still in there, watching me, listening?

My heart drummed at the thought, my chest throbbing with the memory of its pain.

"I have an idea," I said, my heart already drumming faster and my stomach twisted up with dread. "Rook, give me your cannon thing."

"Why?" Rook asked, brown eyes narrowed suspiciously. He was covered in ash, his brown skin literally ashy, and I wondered if I looked as much like a battered ghost.

"Zaba," Kier warned, and I flinched away without meaning to, hearing the same name on the Haar's tongue— so close to Kier's voice but raspier.

"Do you think those things will really take out the Haar?" I asked, avoiding both their stares.

"If Xio says they will, they will," Kier replied, his eyes burning the side of my face even if I wouldn't look at him, my gaze fixed upward instead.

"Alright," I said, taking a deep breath and tensing my muscles.

Before either of them could react I backed up from the wall and took a running jump, catching myself on a windowsill above their heads by my fingertips.

"*Zabaletta!*" Kier growled, a heavy note of panic in his voice.

"I'm fine," I called down, pulling myself up onto the ledge. "Rook, toss me your cannon."

"Not the first time someone's asked me that," Rook quipped with a weak grin, eyeing the distance before drawing his arm back and throwing the big, clunky weapon. I nearly dropped the damn thing, but dug my fingernails into the solid crystal sitting on top of it, and dragged it in towards my body, adjusting my grip.

"I'm coming up after you," Kier seethed.

"Oh, yeah?" I shouted over the deep, ominous creaking from above. "When's the last time you scaled a building?"

"When's the last time *you* scaled a building?" he threw back, definitely panicking.

"An hour ago, give or take a few minutes. I'm a thief and assassin, dear husband. I got this."

But despite my bravado, I felt sick as I peered above the windowsill at the mass of roiling fog, getting more powerful with every inch it gained if the bigger pockmarks it left in the wall were anything to judge by.

"If you wanna do something useful," I called down. "Go find Xiona and get the other two cannons. Shoot the fog when I give the signal."

"What's the signal?" Rook demanded shrilly.

"Don't worry," I replied, tensing my body again. "You won't miss it."

I jammed the cannon down the back of my shirt, making sure it was secure against my spine before I took a deep breath and launched myself up the building. Towards the Haar that could reduce me to bleached bones in a heartbeat.

37

"*H*ey!" I shouted at the Haar, clinging to the side of the castle by my fingertips. "I know you can hear me!"

Great, now I'm shouting at a cloud. And probably about to plummet to my death.

"Get your ass out of that cloud and talk to me, Haar!"

I gritted my teeth and hauled myself up another few inches, digging my fingers into the mortar between grey bricks and climbing torturously slowly. I had to be careful. This wasn't a two-storey house I was scaling, but a damn castle. It was a lot further to fall.

"Haar! Don't ignore me," I screamed with what little breath there was in my lungs.

There was a shrill voice in my head that said I was the world's biggest idiot for doing this. But I had to believe the fog creature was in there, and would listen to me.

"Stop this," I panted, climbing higher and suppressing a shudder when tendrils slithered from the cloud swallowing the top half of the castle, brushing over my knuckles. "You became like this because you lost someone, and now you're *killing* everyone—how does that make sense? Now everyone will know the loss you've felt, and everyone will suffer like you did."

"Everyone will know," it hissed, barely loud enough for me to hear, but my breathing hitched at its faint voice. So it *was* still in there, and listening to me.

That was good, I reminded myself, even as fear made me cold.

"So you want the world to burn because you lost your sister?" I demanded breathily, not letting myself think about that too hard. This was a part of Kier, I had no doubt. "You're wiping out the whole damn kingdom, Haar. There'll be nothing left."

"Lost," it whispered, the tendrils of fog creeping over the back of my hand and winding around my wrist.

I risked falling by shaking off its cold grip, but I refused to get trapped like I had within the ring of fog. Blue magic spat from my ring in response to my strong emotion, but instead of receding, the giant mass of fog surged towards me.

"Oh gods," I choked out in a small voice, my skin crawling with premonitory warning and my grip on the bricks tenuous at best.

I'm going to die here, I thought. What an idiot. I pictured my tombstone: here lies Zabaletta Kollastus, who tried to convince a murderous cloud of fog not to kill everyone, and plummeted to her death.

Wait. Kollastus? Fuck, when had I started taking my married name seriously?

"Not," the Haar said, its raspy voice moving through the fog as it surrounded me on all sides, a thick limb winding around my waist. I didn't miss the fact that I was more stable with its arm keeping me captive, or that I was less likely to fall.

Okay, revised tombstone: here lies Zabaletta Kollastus, hugged to death by a fog cloud.

"Killing everyone," that rough voice went on, its whisper sliding down my senses like a fingernail down a chalkboard. "Not."

"Um, beg to differ, buddy. You ate everyone and left their bones. You turned cities to dust. I've seen it—I was there when you wrecked Cyana. I saw you nearly kill a kid, for fuck's sake. Don't try to bullshit me."

A solid finger stroked down my cheek, and I flinched back. This might have been a part of Kier, but it was creepy as hell, and no matter how bad I felt for the Haar, I wasn't letting it feel me up. No way, no how.

"Lost," it repeated, cold breath rippling down my neck.

I recoiled so hard I lost my grip on the wall, my fingernails scraping stone ineffectively, one second from disaster.

The cloud flooded in around me, turning my whole vision white and silver. I screamed, a sound completely without dignity, and flailed as I hung in mid-air, fog wrapped like solid iron around me.

The cannon slid down the back of my shirt, but by some miracle it didn't fall out.

"Stop this," I rasped. "Enough people have died."

I couldn't see the Haar's body like it had formed before, but I could *feel* it, sense its eyes on me and its attention pinned to me. An echo of its pain throbbed behind my ribs, and I clenched my teeth, trying to fight my way back to the wall. I didn't like being at its mercy one bit.

"Died. No," the Haar rasped, pressing tighter against me, moulding to my body. "Everyone will suffer. No."

I shook my head, freaked out and confused and absolutely *petrified* that the Haar would drop me. Below, blue light flashed through the crowd, as if Kier and Rook were fighting their own Haar adversary.

"What?" I choked out, breathless and squeaky.

"Lost," it said with emphasis.

"Put me somewhere safe," I rasped. "I can't think when I'm going to fall."

"Safe," it agreed, tightening its limbs around me.

That was a hard *no*, then.

My options weren't looking good. I eyed the ground below, and wondered when the hell I'd become so heroic and selfless as I reached my hand behind my back and under my shirt.

"Safe, Zaba."

Sure, floating dangerously fuck knows how many feet in the air, with only a cloud of fog and wild magic to keep me upright ... *definitely* safe.

"No, not safe," I panted, losing air with every second. Trying to buy myself time to reconsider.

But I closed my fingers around the handle of the cannon, its metal cold against my palm.

"You can't keep killing people, no matter how hurt you are at losing your sister. I genuinely like people in this damn kingdom, and I can't let you kill them, too."

"Lost, Zaba, lost," it said, a note of pleading in its voice. "Listen," it hissed in the same tone I'd used to summon it.

"I won't be lost, too," I replied. "And neither will Kier."

Cursing myself the whole damned time, I dragged the cannon from under my shirt, found the trigger with my finger, and before I could second—or tenth—guess myself, I crooked my finger.

Bright blue light erupted through the huge gemstone hulking on top of the cannon, and shot down the barrel so powerfully that I was kicked backwards. I didn't taste fog's ruin on the air; instead, something bitter coated my tongue.

I cried so hard I bruised my throat, but it was drowned out by the awful scream of the Haar. It was so loud my eardrums burst and pain filled my head. I felt like I'd been shot *myself*, pain rampaging from my skull to my chest to the rest of me.

"Sorry," I choked out, but I knew the Haar wouldn't hear me.

I reached out my hand to touch the crumpling cloud in front of me. The fog's ruin shouldn't have hurt the Haar; it should have placated it like it always had. But the Haar *screamed*, and shook around me, losing its grip on my middle.

"This shouldn't be happening," I hissed as the cloud wavered. "I didn't know it would do this!"

I knew it would stop the Haar, figured it would convince it to move somewhere else, but this was pain—a deep and true wound. And I felt it sear across my soul, too.

"No," it breathed, its voice wispy and weak like it had been when it first formed from the wall of fog. "Stop —stop—"

I regretted it. In that split second, as the fog shivered and broke apart, as the Haar screamed for help, I wished I'd let the murderous fog keep hurting people. I was making some seriously questionable life choices lately.

The cloud broke apart until I could see the sky above, until I could see the crumbling roof of the castle and its pockmarked walls, its shattered windows. The fog unravelled until the only thing left was the coil around my waist and the voice whispering around me.

"Stay. I stay," the Haar breathed, barely audible.

"Fuck," I choked out as the final bit of fog finally burned away from around me.

My curse rose into a visceral scream as I fell, tumbling upside down. Hair covered my face, and the castle streaked past at the speed of light. I couldn't spot a handhold, let alone grasp one to save myself.

Letta, you fucking idiot, was my final thought. It was as good a final thought as any.

Air cut at my face, slashing my body as I plummeted, gathering speed. I'd lost the cannon a way back, and now I held only air, not a single hope in the world of stopping my fall.

I'd be lucky if I slammed into the ground and didn't break on the wall, my spine shattering on impact. I didn't want to die in such a public space, on display for ... for *who?* There was no one else. And now I'd be like all the others —lost.

I didn't have enough air for another scream, but a mournful groan rattled my throat as I neared the bottom of the castle, my body tingling in anticipation of the impact—

Sapphire light blasted up from the ground, and I whim- pered in pain as it slammed into me with all the force of a charging bull.

The magic pushed around me and swallowed me whole, pressing over my neck, my mouth, my nose, until I breathed power, until I couldn't move without brushing up against lightning-sharp magic.

I was so disoriented by the feeling of being drowned in magic—sharper and more dangerous than the fog that had swaddled me—that I didn't realise I'd been lowered to the ground until my feet wavered on grass and I toppled into a hard body.

Kier swore in a string of unfamiliar words, gripping me

so tight around my waist that I moaned in pain again. I must have had bruises on every inch of my body.

"Thank the Mother," a welcome voice sighed—Rook. "The Haar's gone."

Xiona scoffed—and rage boiled up in me so fast that I choked on it. "It's not gone. A giant cloud swept out of the city; she just chased off the cloud over the castle."

I whipped out of Kier's arms and swung my fist back, slamming it into Xiona's golden face with a satisfying crunch. My knuckles throbbed, but what was one more ache?

"What the *hell* did you put in those cannons?" I demanded, breathing fast, still rattled from my fall—and the Haar's pain still spiking through my chest. But rage blackened my vision as I faced Xiona. "That was far fucking more than fog's ruin."

She spat blood, baring her teeth at me. "So what?"

"It's *part of Kier,* you thoughtless bitch!" I screamed, my hands shaking even as I lifted them to throw another punch.

Kier caught my wrists, and Rook grabbed Xiona as she launched at me, her blonde hair whipping around her.

"It speaks with *his* voice," I went on, hissing now. "Its body looks scarily close to *his*. It acts like Danette is its own sister. If you kill the Haar, how do you know you won't kill Kier?"

"Shit," Rook breathed, shock in his eyes.

Xiona sneered at me and shoved off her friend's grip, stalking away. "Your days are fucking numbered, traitor," she called over her shoulder, teeth a white flash in her golden face.

"Xio," Kier warned, pressing his hand to my lower back, either to reassure me or restrain me.

Xiona laughed, a twisted dark sound. "You don't even

care that she tried to kill you? Try thinking with your head instead of your cock, Kier!"

"*Alright*," Rook said sharply, sounding more pissed off than I'd heard him with her. "She just took out the Haar and saved our castle; maybe give her a break yeah, Xio?"

Xiona snarled in answer, her skin flashing blue. I inhaled sharply in surprise, but she regained control of herself and didn't shift. I didn't want to show fear, not to her and especially not to Kier and Rook who deserved better than me being afraid of goblins right now.

I didn't even want to think about how relieved I was that I hadn't completely killed the Haar. I pushed all that panic away, revelling in the fact that I was alive and not splattered on the ground.

"Thanks for saving me," I said to Kier, the words quiet and just for him. I turned to look at him, the eye contact making my stomach squirm.

"I was only returning the favour," he replied, dark blue eyes curious as he watched me. "You came for me when the fog trapped me."

I shrugged, self-conscious. "Just being a good human being."

"Mm," he agreed. "I didn't know humans could be good."

"Right back at you with goblins."

"I'm gonna make sure Xio doesn't destroy what's left of the city in her rage," Rook said, walking hastily away. I didn't miss the pointed look he gave me. Right.

I took a fortifying breath. Rook was right, and if I wanted to stay here as anything other than Kier's prisoner, I should probably fess up. Besides, I wanted answers. I wanted to know why he'd killed my sister.

But I didn't know what he'd say, and that scared the hell out of me. This could change the tenuous peace I'd made with him, could poison the fledgling feelings I had for him, and part of me wanted to hang onto them, to not let anything damage them. It was selfish, and there was *no* ignoring what he'd done to Natasya, but ... I wanted him for myself.

The man I hated, my worst enemy, the goblin I'd spent years fantasising of murdering.

"You killed my sister," I blurted out, not daring to look at him. My eyes stayed firmly on the debris-covered ground, pinned to a chunk of grey stone crushing a portrait of one of Kier's ancestors. "That's why I came here, why I married you. Why I tried to..." I flapped my hand, still not looking at him as I indicated slitting his throat.

"That doesn't make sense," Kier replied, confused enough that my heart leapt and hope choked me. If it was someone else, if the witnesses had been wrong and it *wasn't* the goblin prince—or at least not this goblin prince...

I tentatively turned to look at him.

A deep furrow had formed between Kier's blue eyes, his eyes dull with puzzlement. "I can't have killed your sister, Zaba. I can count the number of people I've killed on one hand, and two of those were accidents when my power first manifested."

I trapped my bottom lip between my teeth to stop its wobbling, only speaking when it was steady. "Someone saw you, a witness said it was you."

My heart thumped so fast and hard that I heard it in my ears, a deep whoosh that shut out the cries of people venturing out of the castle to see the damage.

"So all this time, you thought I'd killed your sister," Kier murmured, sympathy thick in his voice. He lifted a hand, framed the side of my face with it, and the touch brought all my roaring vulnerabilities to the surface.

"You're sure?" I pressed, my voice heavy with emotion. "You're absolutely sure? I can't—I *can't* have planned all this time, put everything I have into this—"

Five years of my life wasted. Even if it had brought me here, to Kier, to my mate ... all that time was wasted.

"You never met Natasya Stellara? You've never been to Seagrave?" I pressed.

I couldn't say what exactly changed on Kier's face. It was a glacial shift, a wall built around his emotions, a shutter over his eyes. His hand lowered from my face and my bottom lip trembled.

Gods, no. Please. *Please.*

I'd only ever wanted one thing—revenge. But now I wanted him. I wanted *him*, gods dammit, and there was only one reason he'd be stepping back and looking at me like that —cold, reassessing.

"Kier," I choked out, wrapping my arms around myself, hands shaking.

There was nothing familiar in his face, nothing even remotely like the Kier I'd grown to know this month. Even the bitter, begrudging man who'd stood across from me on our wedding day had been warmer than the stone that faced me now.

"You're from Seagrave."

Flat words, with no feeling in them. But I sensed his rage, boiling up inside him. It lodged behind my ribs, right beside the Haar's pain, so strong that it felt like my own fury.

"So it *was* you," I whispered, but I couldn't summon the desire to kill him anymore. *I fucked up, Natasya. You deserve justice, but I can't do this.* "Why?"

I hated how small my voice was. I wished Rook had stayed.

Kier took a sudden step towards me, and I backed up, breathless. A minute ago he'd been touching me with fondness, talking softly, thanking me for saving his life. Now he looked at me like I was dead to him, nothing more than dirt on his shoe.

"You really should have killed me when you had the chance, Zabaletta Stellara," he said coldly. "You'll never get another chance."

"I don't want one," I tried to snarl, but I could barely whisper it.

I backed up another step, shaking all over. He'd called me Stellara— not Kollastus. It had no right to hurt as much as it did.

"Just tell me why."

"Your spiteful bitch of a sister," Kier spat, emotion finally sparking in his voice as he glared at me, "stole the gem of power that kept my ten-year-old sister alive."

I flinched back another step—not from his rage, but from his words.

Natasya had ... *why?* That didn't make any sense. Why would she? I shook my head, denying it. She'd never do that to a kid. Never. I wasn't much older than Danette had been then; Natasya would never do that.

Kier smiled, baring his teeth in warning. "You don't believe me? Your sister was part of a group of rebels who went against your human military's rules, sneaking past our army into our civilian areas to strike us harder, using far cruller methods."

Cold crept through me. Secret lawbreaking, ignoring authority, sneaking around ... that all sounded like my sister. Add in that she thought she was saving our people from goblins and ... yeah, I could see that.

"She'd never hurt a kid," I argued, the one thing I could hold onto. She'd never do that. That wasn't Natasya.

I gulped at the sneer on Kier's face as he looked at me. Who *was* this? This wasn't the Kier I knew, wasn't the Kier I was falling in sickening, hateful love with.

"She thought it was powering our armies, giving them an edge against your people." The hate he fuelled into those two words—your people—made my breath catch. "So she led a trio of rebels into my home, and they stole the stone while we slept. She murdered *my baby sister*," Kier growled, so deep that a sob caught in my throat.

His skin rippled, blue flashing through dark tan. I curled my hands into fists to stop them shaking, backing up another step and crying out when a chunk of stone hit my heel, sending me onto my ass on the ground. Pain shot up my tailbone, and I panted for breath, realising with horror that there were tears on my cheeks.

"I only have your word for this," I choked out, gasping for breath. "You're a liar."

Kier smiled cruelly as he loomed over me. "You are the liar, *wife*. You pretended to be my dutiful spouse and all the while you planned to kill me."

"You deserve it!" I spat. "What you did to Natasya..."

"No less than she deserved for what *she* did to my sister," Kier snarled right back at me, teeth bared and needle-thin. If he ripped out my throat with those things, it'd probably hurt less than my broken heart right now.

"She'd never have done it if she'd known," I defended her, but weakly. *Fuck, Natasya, what did you do...?* "She wouldn't hurt a kid, no matter their species. But you—you *chose* to do everything you did to Natasya. Every cut—"

I jerked my head to the side and vomited in the ash, bile burning my throat.

He'd done it; he'd really killed my sister. All this time, I'd been holding onto the pathetic hope that someone else had killed her. From the moment he said he'd never been on a battlefield, I'd managed to convince myself it hadn't been him.

Tears stabbed my eyes harder. I wiped my mouth with the back of my hand, feeling like utter shit.

"Get out of my city," Kier ordered, glaring down at me. "Get out of the whole damn kingdom."

My stomach cramped and my heart squeezed at the same time. I swore even my soul flinched.

I pushed shakily to my feet. "I found a way to accept it," I rasped. "What you did. Who you were. Even with that, I found a way to accept you, to accept that you're my mate."

Kier's laugh was a beautiful weapon. It cut so deep that I pressed a hand to my chest to check for blood. "I'm no such thing."

"I won't go," I rasped, thick with tears. "You can't make me."

I couldn't explain why I wanted to stay, but there was no denying it. I didn't want to leave, especially not like this. Kier was right; I should have killed him when I had the chance, because now I had to live with all of this. There would never be a moment when it didn't hurt.

The hate in Kier's eyes gouged into my chest when he smirked. "But I *can* make you," he disagreed. "Zabaletta Stellara, I renounce you as my wife and exile you from Lazankh. Should you return, my guard will have instructions to execute you on sight."

"You can't do this," I gasped, panic and rage twisting together inside me. "It doesn't work like that, you bastard," I snarled. "You don't just get to renounce me. We signed papers, we gave vows, there was a damn *priest*."

Kier laughed, so low it was little more than thunder. "We're in goblin lands now, Zabaletta. I can do whatever I want here."

"We got married in the human lands. Nice try, asshole."

He took a threatening step toward me, and between one step and the next, tanned skin became icy blue. His ears grew longer, sharper, his shoulders broadened, arms became as thick as tree trunks, and his hands grew massive enough to snap me. He was seven foot tall, every part of his body a visible threat.

He was still recognisably Kier, his features the same and hair still long and black, but he snapped his razor teeth at me, and I scrambled away, primal fear quickening my heart-beat and wrecking my breathing.

"You're exiled," he growled, voice so much deeper in this form. "You have one hour to leave my city before I rip you to shreds, too."

The *too* in that sentence made me see red, and sapphire magic flashed from my ring. But it died as fast as it rose, leaving me alone with Kier in goblin form and enough hurt to fill a quarry.

"You're a monster," I said, my voice far weaker than I wanted it to be. "Not because of this." I waved a hand at his goblin-ness. "Because of what you did to Natasya. I wouldn't want to stay anywhere near you anyway. I'm happy to leave."

All lies, delivered with venom and enough cruelty to match Kier's.

"I hope you suffer for the rest of your life," I added with a twisted smile, and forced myself to walk away.

Every step killed me, a sharp pain in my chest that seemed to drag me backwards. I fought through it, ignoring the hot tears on my cheeks. I didn't know where to go, didn't know how to get out of this kingdom and back to the human lands, and no one would help me when they found out my sister had killed their princess.

Worst of all, I had no revenge to keep me fighting. I'd missed my only shot. But after finding out what Natasya had done, accidentally or not, I wasn't sure Kier deserved to die. He really was a monster, a twisted, fucked up man with a hidden cruelty I hadn't seen coming. But part of me understood, and I hated it. The only difference between Kier and me was he'd actually got revenge, and I'd failed.

I shoved a hand to my mouth like it could trap the sob that came crashing up my throat.

A door squeaked open at the bottom of a wrecked building, a pale blue head poking out and checking to see the fog was gone. Part of me wished the Haar had taken me with it, wherever it had gone off to now. At least then I wouldn't be alone.

"Your highness?" a soft female voice asked, the woman peering at me as I dragged myself down the street towards the gates. "Are you alright?"

There were a hundred ways I could answer. *I'm pretty sure I've been stripped of my title. I've never been less alright than right now. I think I fell in love with my worst enemy. My sister did something unforgivable and I'm not sure how to cope with it. I don't want to leave.*

"No," I whispered, not sure the woman could even hear me as I kept putting one foot in front of the other. "I'm lost."

THANK you for reading - we hope you loved Letta and Kier! We're so grateful for the support you guys have shown this series so far! Letta's story will continue in The Doomed Prince, which you can pre-order now!

While you wait, Leigh Kelsey has a RH fantasy romance series you can read. Start the series with Heir of Ruin for sexy fae, enemies to lovers, fated mates, a badass princess, and enough sarcasm and tawdry ballads to fill an inn on the wrong side of town.

THANK YOU FOR READING!

Need the next book ASAP? Let me know – the more demand for a series, the more likely we are to bump the next book to the top of our list!

Reviews make the world go 'round - or at least they do in our world. If you loved this book and you can spare a minute, please leave a review on Amazon or wherever else you like to review. Even the smallest, one-line review has an impact, and helps us reach new readers like you awesome people.

Thank you to everyone who's already reviewed. Your words mean we can keep writing the books you love!

FOUR FREEBIES FOR YOU

Fancy some freebies? Leigh will send you three when you join my newsletter! I promise never to spam you, and I rarely send more frequently than once a fortnight so you won't be overloaded with emails.

Join here: http://bit.ly/LeighKelseyNL

JOIN LEIGH'S READER GROUP!

Join my reader group for news, giveaways, and exclusives!

To get news about upcoming releases before anywhere else, and early access to my books, come join my Leigh Kelsey's Paranormal Den group over on Facebook!

ABOUT LEIGH

Leigh Kelsey is the author of sweet, psycho, steamy books for anyone with a soft spot for steely women and the tortured men who love them. No matter what stories she's writing – vampires or shifters, psychos or rebels – they all share a common thread of romance, heart, and action.

She is the author of Killer Crescent, The Broken Alphas series, Shadowfire Mates, and the Lili Kazana series, among others. Find her MF dark romance books under the name Phoebe Ash.

FIND THESE OTHER BOOKS BY LEIGH KELSEY!

All solo books free on Kindle Unlimited

Fae of the Saintlands series

(Enemies To Lovers RH Romance)

Heir of Ruin

Heart of Thorns

Kiss of Iron

Touch of Darkness

A Feud So Dark And Lovely series

(Enemies to Lovers Fantasy MF Romance)

The Goblin's Bride

The Doomed Prince (Coming soon!)

Broken Alphas series

(Complete Rejected Mates Dark Paranormal RH)

The Omega's Wolves

The Omega's Mates

Alpha Knights MC series

(Dark Omegaverse Biker MF)

Guardian

Warning

Killers and Kings series

(Twisted Paranormal Demon RH)
Crazed Candy (August 2022)

Rebels and Psychos Duet
(Complete Twisted Paranormal RH Romance)
Killer Crescent
Blood Wolf

Shadowfire Mates/Blacktower Prison series
(Complete Dragon Shifter Romance series)
Complete Series Box Set
Start with Prison of Embers

Lili Kazana series
(Complete RH Angel/Demon Romance series)
Complete Series Box Set
Start with Cast From Heaven

Vampire Game series
(Complete RH Vampire Romance series)
Complete Series Box Set
Start with Vampire Game

Moonlight Inn series
(Complete Wolf Shifter RH series)
Complete Series Box Set
Start with Mated

Second Breath Academy series
(Complete Paranormal Academy RH series)

How To Raise The Dead

How To Kill A Shadow

How To Banish Evil

Stand Alone Stories

Sinful Beauty (RH Demon Romance Stand-Alone)

ABOUT LYSANDRA

Lysandra Glass is a fantasy romance author from the UK. After falling in love with too many dark, brooding fictional men, she now writes her own stories full of forbidden romance, enemies who fall in love, and vast fantasy worlds teeming with goblins, fae, and elves. Her debut book, The Goblin's Bride, is out now!

FIND THESE OTHER BOOKS BY LYSANDRA GLASS!

All books free on Kindle Unlimited

A Feud So Dark And Lovely series

(Enemies to Lovers Fantasy Romance)

The Goblin's Bride

The Doomed Prince (Coming soon!)

COMING SOON:

Song of Embers series

(Enemies to Lovers Fantasy Romance)

Night of Lapis and Gold

Made in United States
Orlando, FL
11 August 2022

20905791R00161